"Love is complicated. When it ends, it's even more so."

Rebecca squeezed her eyes shut, as if looking in instead of out.

She was a soft touch. Hers was a goodness that didn't come and go, but remained when the going got tough. She was no holiday Christian. It was his guess that she had a big, forgiving heart.

When she opened her eyes, she gave another shoulder shrug. "My sisters tell me that's part of healing and moving on. But this love thing is painful."

"It can be," Chad answered. "So, this guy, he's the one you were hoping to marry?"

"Not exactly. I was just hoping, is all. And now I'm on a path I didn't expect."

"Maybe it's a better one."

"Maybe." She smiled at him, truly smiled.

Just like that his heart clicked, and he was in like with her. How about that?

Books by Jillian Hart

Love Inspired

Heaven Sent
*His Hometown Girl
A Love Worth Waiting For
Heaven Knows
*The Sweetest Gift
*Heart and Soul
*Almost Heaven
*Holiday Homecoming
*Sweet Blessings
For the Twins' Sake
*Heaven's Touch
*Blessed Vows
*A Handful of Heaven
*A Soldier for Christmas
*Precious Blessings
*Every Kind of Heaven
*Everyday Blessings
*A McKaslin Homecoming
**A Holiday To Remember
*Her Wedding Wish
*Her Perfect Man

*The McKaslin Clan

Love Inspired Historical

*Homespun Bride
*High Country Bride

JILLIAN HART

makes her home in Washington State, where she has lived most of her life. When Jillian is not hard at work on her next story, she loves to read, go to lunch with her friends and spend quiet evenings with her family.

Her Perfect Man
Jillian Hart

Steeple
Hill®

Published by Steeple Hill Books™

STEEPLE HILL BOOKS

Steeple
Hill®

ISBN-13: 978-0-373-81369-8
ISBN-10:   0-373-81369-4

HER PERFECT MAN

Copyright © 2008 by Jill Strickler

www.SteepleHill.com

Printed in U.S.A.

But as for me, I will always have hope;
I will praise you more and more.
—*Psalms* 71:14

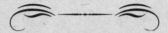

Chapter One

The phone was ringing inside her apartment, but Rebecca McKaslin stepped out into the late-summer evening anyway. Thank goodness for caller ID. Why was Chris calling? He knew she wouldn't talk to him ever again— mostly because she'd told him so. How many times would she have to let it ring before he got a clue?

Exasperated, she yanked the door shut and the lock gave a metallic click. See, this was the reason she'd adopted her newly instated No Man policy. Men, they didn't call when you wanted them to, but when you didn't want them to call *ever,* then, voilà, the phone rang off the hook.

Well, she was a free and independent woman these days and she wasn't even going to let the thought of her ex-boyfriend bug her. It was too bad that he had regrets, because she didn't, thank you very much. She went to hike her purse strap higher on her shoulder—

Wait. No purse strap.

No purse. How had she forgotten it? It was right there by the door on the little hallway table where the phone had been ringing with Chris's number flashing away.

No biggie, she told herself and lifted her hand to sort through her keys.

Wait. No keys. She stared at her empty hand. Had she left her key ring inside, too? Oh, probably. Talk about being an airhead, Rebecca. If she wasn't careful, she was going to turn into her sister Ava who, as adorable as she was, forgot everything.

Okay, this was a major problem. How was she going to drive the car? Pick up the pizza? Get to her sister's house in time to babysit?

Good-going, Rebecca. Way to start off the evening. She folded a stray lock of brown hair out of her eyes. She tried the doorknob just in case it wasn't really locked and that click had been a figment of her imagination.

Nope. The knob didn't turn. Wasn't that just her luck? If she had her purse, she would have her cell phone and so a quick call to someone in her family would fix this in a jiffy. If it wasn't after five o'clock on a Friday, she could bother her neighbor Ephraim, but he was off at a church function.

So who did that leave? Asking a neighbor she didn't know to borrow a phone? She hadn't lived in this complex long. She didn't know her neighbors, other than Ephraim, but she was going to have to start knocking on doors. As she was shy, that was not something she was looking forward to. Although judging by the quiet stillness of the complex, most of them probably wouldn't be home.

On a brighter note, the phone inside her apartment had stopped ringing. Was Chris finally giving up? Getting a hint? Finding a clue?

A girl could always hope. Because she was done with dudes for good—or at least the next decade. Prince Charming could come walking around the corner and she would be Fort Knox. Her affections impenetrable. Her No Man policy was unshakable.

"You need any help?" A man's voice came out of nowhere right behind her.

Her heart jumped hard enough to make it to the moon and back. She turned around and clutched the porch rail to steady herself. There was a drop-dead handsome guy standing on her walkway—and not just everyday ordinary handsome, either. But twenty on a scale of ten. Really wow. She *had* to be dreaming, right? She blinked, but nope, the gorgeous guy was still standing there as real as could be.

He was a big athletic-looking guy—not heavily muscled, but not lanky, either. He was tall with blond hair and a wholesome, guy-next-door grin. He wore a loose sport T-shirt and basketball shorts. Friendly looking.

"I saw you lock yourself out." He had a wholesome smile, too, one that brought out a dimple in his right cheek and an honest sparkle in his dark eyes. He was also carrying a cardboard box in the crook of his arm. "I wasn't peeping or anything. I was unloading my truck and I couldn't help noticing. I'm moving in next door."

"Oh, you're Ephraim's new roommate?"

"Guilty. You must be Rebecca. He's talked about you. Only good things, though. Said to look you up if I wanted to join a Bible study group."

"I'd be happy to give you the information, except—"

"All your information is inside?"

"Yep."

"Isn't that always how it goes?" He flashed her a hundred-watt grin. "You look like you're on your way somewhere."

"Yep, in a hurry without the keys to start my car."

"That's gotta spell trouble." He was, as her sister Ava would say, super-duper.

But was she noticing? No. It was good to know her No Man policy was firmly in place. Talk about peace of mind. She crossed her arms over her heart like a shield. "Trouble? That's the least of it. I'm running late, and now this. It's just been one of those days of doom."

"Hey, I have those too now and then."

There was something about that friendly smile, Rebecca decided as she found herself smiling back. If there really was a Prince Charming, then this man would be him.

"A pretty girl like you is probably rushing out for a date, right?"

"I'm pleading the fifth on that one."

"I see." His voice was warm as if it was a smile all on its own. "I'm Chad, by the way. Chad Lawson."

"Rebecca McKaslin."

"Well, Rebecca. Do you have a spare key lying around?"

"No. I'm not that organized." Mostly because she wasn't usually this absent-minded. "And if I did, I wouldn't be standing here staring like I've lost my mind."

"That's not how I would describe you."

"Then you are too kind." She shaded her eyes with her hand. "I hate to bother you, but could I use your phone?"

"That would be no bother at all." There went that dimple, flashing at her. He had the knack of putting people at ease. "You're going to call a locksmith?"

"Or my sister for the key. It's her condo. I rent from her. She's not going to be happy with me. Katherine is pregnant and on bed rest."

"Is she going to be okay?"

Rebecca sighed. Right now she should start collecting all the reasons why she wasn't going to like Chad, but then he had to go and ask the perfect question. She had to like anyone who asked about her family. "It looks as if she and the baby will be fine, but you never know. It's some high blood pressure problem."

"I'll keep her in my prayers." He seemed sincere standing there with the sunlight bronzing him and concern on his chiseled face. "You don't want to disturb her by getting that key. I've got an idea."

"What kind of idea?" This ought to be interesting. She squinted at him, trying to figure out why he was being so nice. Maybe he was just a nice guy—or liked people to think he was. A smart girl would be on guard for that kind of thing.

"How about I break in for you?"

"Break in? Uh, that has the word *break* in it."

"Sure, but not literally." There was something reassuring about him as he set down the cardboard box he carried on the concrete walkway. "I'm assuming that your unit has a sliding-glass door like ours does?"

"Sure, but—"

"Then trust me."

Wow, he had the most honest eyes. Good thing there wasn't a single bit of interest. Nada. Zero on a scale of ten.

"Wait here. I'll be right back." He had classic features, a confident rugged air to him, tousled blond hair and wide shoulders. In short: gorgeous.

Didn't that spell trouble?

Not for me, she reminded herself. She wanted to find fault with him but she couldn't. She didn't want to like the way two dimples bracketed his friendly, open smile or the dependable line of his wide shoulders as he turned and disappeared around the corner of her condo.

Was he a locksmith or something? She checked her watch; she had called in a pizza order for pickup and it was probably about ready. She didn't want the cheesy sticks to dry out. How long did it take for a locksmith to pick a lock, or whatever it was that they did?

She tried not to think about how disappointed little Tyler was going to be if they didn't have the pizza night she'd promised him. Hey, she was going to be disappointed, too, because she loved her nights with the munchkins. Family was everything to her. Simply everything.

The warm wind gusted gently, bringing the scent of roses from the garden around back. She let the fragrance wash through her. Just the sweet old-fashioned scent soothed her. Why was she so tense?

It wasn't only from Chris's barrage of calls. He'd done this before when they were off again. She was managing through the stress. It would stop, if all went according to her experience with him. No, what bothered her was much more complex, and it troubled her every time she sat still long enough to feel it.

She ought to be moving forward with her

life instead of being stuck in place. Everything felt off. She hated feeling like this, lost and at loose ends. Why was it still bugging her? Hadn't she come to a good solution last night in prayer?

Yes. She was letting go and letting God.

Another phone started to ring again—she recognized the electronic jingle of her cell phone muffled by the thick door. No doubt it was Chris again, persistent, as always.

I'm giving this up to you, too, Lord. She looked heavenward and heard the phone cut off—and start ringing again. Not the best of signs, but her faith was strong. *I trust You with this. I know You have a plan.*

And speaking of a plan, where had the neighbor guy gone? There wasn't one sign of Chad. Then again, there wasn't the sound of breaking glass, either. That had to be a good thing.

Suddenly her doorknob rattled and turned. She startled in surprise as the door swung open to reveal Chad standing in her foyer.

"What? How did you—" She leaned against the rail as he joined her on the porch. "What did you do?"

"I went to your patio and popped open the sliding-glass door."

That fazed her. "But it was locked."

"Yep. Don't worry, your door doesn't have a scratch on it."

"But how did you open it?"

"Trade secret. I used to work summers for my uncle. He owns a glass shop." Chad shrugged those wonderful shoulders of his. Washed in sunlight and charm, he looked like a wholesome, decent man. "You really should get a dowel for the track. That will keep burglars from doing the same thing I did."

"Great. I feel so much better knowing that."

His eyes had a nice, friendly sparkle to go along with his killer grin. The more handsome a guy, the more trouble he was. Chris had been gorgeous and look how that had turned out. She hated to generalize, because her sisters had all married hunky men and they were as happy as clams. She was happy for them.

She didn't have that kind of luck.

"I locked the sliding door, so you don't have to worry about it." He loped down the steps.

"So that's it? You're just walking off, your good deed done, and now you're going back to your unpacking?"

"That was my plan." He turned around and backed down the walk. "I don't want to make you late. You're obviously on your way somewhere. A girl like you has a boyfriend, doesn't she?"

"And what exactly is that supposed to mean?" She didn't want him to know the truth, so she gave him The Eye, as her brother called it. "A girl like me?"

"Pretty. Together. Smart."

"You are a shameless flatterer. My last boyfriend talked like you at first. He was good with compliments, but not so good with kindness and respect and following his Christian values, or so I found out."

"Hey, I don't want to pay for his mistakes." He came to a stop at the curb and winked at her. "I'm perfectly innocent."

"No guy is perfectly innocent."

"Well, you got me there, but I'm living my faith. My Christian values." He wanted to be clear about that. She's all right, he thought, and he liked that she made him laugh. He'd had a long day and a tough one. It felt good to smile. "You let me know if you need anything else. I'll be happy to come to your rescue."

"Like that's a comforting thought. I'm trying to stay out of trouble." She had happy eyes and a mouth that said she smiled often.

He liked that, too.

She was really lovely with those delicate features and heart-shaped face and the sleek, dark fall of her brown hair. It was hard to miss the gold cross dangling on a fine chain around her neck.

Faith was important to him, too. "You haven't answered my question. If you're not going on a date, then where are you headed?"

"And that's your business, because...?" She arched one slim eyebrow at him, as if she were taking careful note of his personality flaws.

He wasn't fooled. Not one bit. He'd been inside her place. Sure, he'd noticed the cross-stitch that was sitting half-finished on the coffee table, and the Bible and devotional on the kitchen table. He wasn't snooping, but a guy couldn't help noticing. It wasn't as if he could close his eyes and not see anything, right?

"It's not my business," he had to admit. "Just curious."

"Didn't curiosity get the cat into trouble?" She slipped through the door.

"Who said I wasn't trouble?"

"Yep, that's just what I thought about you." She grabbed her purse and keys and shut the door. "I'm babysitting for my other sister and her husband. They have a date night tonight."

"That's nice you do that for her. So family's important to you."

"Absolutely. What about you?" She squinted at him. "It's only fair that *you* answer a question. How do you know Ephraim?"

"He and I have been summer buddies since we were six."

"Summer buddies?" she asked with a quizzical look as she turned the dead bolt.

"When my mom and dad wanted to get rid of me for the summer, they sent me to my aunt and uncle's." He saw the question forming on her expressive face and kept talking; he tried not to mention his parents if he could help it. Too complicated, too painful, too everything. "Ephraim lived next door to Uncle Calvin. He came over and offered me a Popsicle and the rest, as they say, was history."

He liked the way she seemed to be in a good mood, even on a day of doom, as she'd claimed. She had the prettiest sparkles in her cinnamon-brown eyes that shimmered with warmth and humor.

"A Popsicle tends to cement the important relationships," she said. "Especially a grape one."

He chuckled, his heart just…feeling. He

didn't know how to describe it, only that it was nice. Real nice. "That's where I've been wrong in the past. I neglected to offer a Popsicle."

"A fatal mistake."

She was one of those totally organized girls who seemed completely together. Although she was dressed casually, everything was coordinated and that purse she had over her shoulder was no cheap knockoff. His aunt had one almost like it. That, along with her spring-sunshine goodness, made Rebecca McKaslin an awesome combination. She slipped her keys into the outside pocket on her purse and descended the steps like a cool breeze.

He really should go. So why weren't his feet taking him farther down the walk? "How old are your nieces or nephews?"

"Isn't it my turn to ask the questions?" She dug her sunglasses out of her purse. "Are you serious about the Bible study group?"

"Wouldn't have asked if I wasn't."

"Why aren't you going to Ephraim's group?" She slipped the glasses on, pausing to study him hard for any obvious flaws. She really wanted to find some flaws.

"I have obligations on Friday evenings."

"A girlfriend?" Now, why did she ask that?

She was teasing him, because he'd been just a tad curious about her. She leaned through the doorway to grab the bag she always carried to church with her. Inside was the flyer with all the group's specifics. She handed it to him, realizing he was blushing.

Blushing. She didn't know guys did that. Maybe the decent ones did. What did she know?

"Uh—" He looked flustered. "Currently, no."

"See how personal that question can be?"

"I do. You're making a point."

"Yes. You are a smart guy." She decided that a guy whose ears turned pink when asked about a girlfriend had to be okay. "Will I see you there?"

"Count on it." He waved the flyer for confirmation.

"Good, our group has been losing numbers lately. A lot of us graduated last May. Well, I've got a pizza waiting."

"Pizza. Sounds good. Is it for your niece? Nephew?"

"One of each."

"Must be nice to have family." He joined her on the walk, his gait easy and athletic, his voice amicable.

"It is." She paused at the end of the walkway, where the sidewalk would take her left to the driveway, where her car was parked. "I don't know what I'd do without my family. I have one older brother and five older sisters."

"Sounds like heaven to me. I'm an only kid."

"Was that a little lonely growing up?"

"Sometimes."

It was hard not to feel for him. "As a kid, I always had someone looking out for me and someone to do things with. I was hardly ever alone. It's probably why I like spending so much time alone now."

"I pretty much had to figure things out for myself when I was little." He knelt to grab his box of books. It was packed with what looked like mysteries. Though it had to be heavy, he lifted the box with ease.

So he was a serious reader. That didn't surprise her one bit. He looked nearly perfect standing in the golden brush of the light, with the gentle breeze ruffling his blond hair and an expression of seriousness on his face. Why, she suspected if her sister Ava were to drive up right now she would call him a Mr. Wishable.

Worse, she would probably go on to call him Mr. Right, and there was no way he could be that. Knowing her luck, she had probably missed the boat to Mr. Right and would be forever standing on the dock. "It was good to meet you, Chad Lawson. I'll see you on Wednesday night."

"Definitely." He folded up the flyer and slipped it into his book box. "Have a good time with your niece and nephew."

"I will. Tyler's five, he's total fun, and the two-year-old keeps me on my toes." Why wasn't she leaving? You're late, late, late, Rebecca. So exactly why was she lingering, as if she didn't want to go? "Good luck with the moving. It's a special kind of torture. I hope it goes all right."

"Thanks. I'm lucky that I packed light, but it's still a pain."

"Did I say thanks for stopping to help me out? I can't remember if I did."

"You did."

"Good. Forgive me, I'm more scattered than usual. I'm not normally like this. Goodbye, Chad."

"Bye." As if she was ever scattered at all, he thought, dismissing her self-deprecating sense of humor. He watched her saunter over to her little red Honda parked in the driveway in front of her closed garage door.

The car suited her, zippy and fun and cute all at once.

Yep, she was real nice.

The sun's heat beat down on him, and he realized it was getting late and the box he was holding was getting heavier. He resisted the urge to give Rebecca one last look as her car backed slowly out of the driveway. But as he headed for his apartment, he thought of her.

Chapter Two

"Rebba?"

Madison wobbled into the TV's glare. The little girl was pure sweetness with her light brown curls, big wide eyes and pixie's face. Tonight she wore her pink-and-purple Cinderella pajamas and a sleepy frown.

Rebecca was out of the chair in a second, scooping up the warm, sleep-snuggly toddler into her arms. "What is it, princess?"

"Thirsty." A huge yawn, and then both little arms wrapped around Rebecca's neck. "Where's Mommy?"

"She's still out with your daddy." Rebecca started for the kitchen. "Let's get you that water and put you right back to bed."

"I want Daddy."

"I know you do, princess." She opened the

cupboard door with one hand, found the pink cup with the princesses on it and turned on the tap. The water was nice and cold and she filled the cup partway. "He'll be home before you know it."

"Ye-ah." Madison sighed, clearly missing her parents. Hers was a loving and secure world. Heaven knew that Danielle and her husband, Jonas, did everything they could to ensure that for their kids.

As she held the cup to her niece's lips and tipped it so she could drink in dainty little sips, Rebecca had to wonder. Would her life have turned out differently if her biological dad had been a good man? She had been wondering this a lot lately. The breakup and the man Chris turned out to be was still troubling her.

She'd been younger than Madison was now when her real dad had walked out on the family after beating her mom so badly that she'd been in the hospital for weeks.

Poor Mom. That time was nothing but a scary, hazy blur to Rebecca. She had been too young to understand, but she could see her big sister Danielle standing between her and their rage-filled father. Nearly a lifetime later, she could still hear her mom's broken sobs and the wounded sound she made, lying so still in the corner.

A year later, Mom had married John McKaslin, changing their lives for the better forever. John—who she thought of as her real dad—was a great blessing. Since the day she'd stepped foot in his house, she'd been as safe and secure as Madison was now. She hadn't gained just a great dad, but also a big brother and loving older sisters who couldn't have been more wonderful to her.

"Done?" she asked when the sleepy toddler pushed the cup away.

"I want Minnie." She rubbed her eyes with both little fists.

"She's probably in bed waiting for you." Rebecca set the cup on the counter and gave her niece a smacking kiss on her plump cheek. "Want to go see?"

"O-o-o-kaay." Madison yawned again.

What a cutie. Rebecca held her little niece snug, weaving through the dark house by memory. As she passed by her nephew's bedroom door, she caught sight of him asleep in his bed. He and his dog were faintly graced by the glow of his night-light. He was a cutie, too. She padded down the hall.

Madison gave a tired whine at the sight of her bunny tucked neatly under the covers. Minnie's head and ears were dark against the pale pillowcase.

"See?" Rebecca lowered the child into her bed. "I told you Minnie was waiting for you."

Eyes drooping, head bobbing, Madison reached out to gather her favorite stuffed animal into her chubby arms, snuggled close and was half-asleep before her head touched the pillow. Rebecca smoothed the girl's flyaway curls, and Madison sort of smiled through her sleepiness, slipping away to sweeter dreams.

Yep, Rebecca thought as her heart filled. A total cutie.

It was a pleasure to tuck the little girl's covers around her and tiptoe to the door. The throbbing blue light from the distant TV made the hallway feel surreal, as if this was but a dream, a vision of what she'd always wanted for herself.

Those things were so far away now. Okay, it was her decision to institute a No Man policy and that was great because it kept her heart safe. But at the same time it felt as if time were slipping by. She'd been so busy racing to grow up, enjoying her college years and then hoping her relationship with Chris would lead her to a life like this.

It hadn't, and now she felt empty in the pit of her stomach and in the chambers of her heart. Even in her soul, she felt alone.

She wasn't alone. She knew that as surely as she knew there was a floor at her feet. Her faith was rock solid, her family an un-breakable support and yet she felt hollow, as if she were missing a great part of herself.

No, she corrected, she was missing these dreams of children and marriage, of home and a future.

She checked again on Tyler, who slept on his side facing the wall so all she could see of him was tufts of brown hair and his Dal-matian asleep on the foot of his bed. Lucky lifted his head a few inches and his tail thumped against the blankets as if to say, "No worries. I'm keeping watch."

She wandered back to the TV, hardly noticing the hospital drama flashing across the screen. The sound was low so as not to disturb the kids, and she could barely hear the dialogue. She settled onto the couch as her mind drifted back over the day. She resisted the urge to go dig in her bag to check her cell phone, with the ringer off. She guessed that

Chris had probably called a half-dozen times. Should she deal with it now, or wait until later?

Later, she thought as she grabbed the remote and hit the off button. Definitely later. What was really calling her name was the triple-chocolate cream pie Danielle had left for dessert. Whatever the trouble, didn't chocolate always make it better?

She was plating a nice creamy piece when she heard the garage door crank open. It sounded as though Danielle and Jonas were home. Sure enough, a few minutes later the two of them came through the door. The security system chimed their arrival. It was simple to tell by the happiness on her sister's face that they'd had a good time. Jonas, leaning tiredly on his cane, gave her a nod of thanks, a kind "good-night" and headed down the hall, no doubt to check on the kids.

Danielle set her purse on the end of the counter. "Would you mind cutting me one of those?"

"I've got a plate right here." She knew her sister well and her weakness for chocolate. "You didn't have dessert tonight?"

"Dinner was so good, I didn't save any room." Dani headed to the fridge and took out a gallon of milk. "The movie was great, though. It was about a pair of cops. Jonas really enjoyed all the action."

"He misses his old job." In an instant, things could change in a person's life. Life happened and sometimes it was never the same. Take Jonas for example. Over a year ago, he'd been doing his job as a state trooper and got shot on a routine traffic stop. His life and Dani's had taken a new direction they never expected.

"Yes," Danielle answered sadly. "He loves staying home with the kids and being a full-time dad, but he misses being a trooper, too."

God had been gracious. Jonas was doing fine and their family was stronger than ever, but it hadn't been easy. Life gave a person a certain amount of battle scars. Although she hadn't gone through anything nearly as traumatic as Jonas had, she had her own emotional scars.

What she'd gone through with Chris and his final battle, as she thought of it, had been life changing for her. And if her big brother, Spence, hadn't come to her rescue, she hated to think what would have happened. She wondered where she would be right now if she hadn't met Chris.

"You seem a million miles away." Danielle took two glasses down from the cupboard and began filling them. "You get that troubled look when Chris has been bothering you. Has he been calling?"

"He's started up again. You know how he does."

"I do. Have you answered?"

"No, and I'm avoiding his calls because I know he wants to start things up again."

"And you don't want that, right?"

"Right. Don't worry. I'm through with Chris. I'm through with men. I'm going to be just fine." She gave a generous piece of pie to her sister. "Does Jonas want any?"

"No. He's pretty tired and besides, he's a gem about leaving us girls to talk."

"He's pretty great to you." Rebecca took two forks from the drawer.

"I know. I thank God for him every day." Warm and loving and totally devoted to her husband—that was Danielle. "You didn't answer my question, you know."

"Sorry. I've just got a lot on my mind." And there it was, what she'd been trying not to think about all evening: her mess of a life.

"We can talk about it. Maybe I can help. Or maybe we can try to brainstorm. There have got to be some great single men out there that you can date." Danielle carried the milk back to the fridge, and in the wan light from inside the door she looked exceptionally pale and tired.

There had been a lot on her shoulders when Jonas had first been hurt, but now that he was much better, Danielle was back to her old self. Except for tonight.

"Forget my problems," she said. "I should be asking you if you're okay."

"I'm fine." Danielle closed the fridge door and waved away her concern.

"You don't look like you're getting enough sleep or something. I work until four tomorrow, but I can come by after and help out. Maybe make dinner for you?"

"That's great of you, Becca, but it's not necessary." She took both glasses to the table. "I'm just a little tired. I'm still adjusting to working full-time is all."

"Are you sure?" She followed her sister, plates in hand.

"Positive." Danielle had taken a management job at their family's bookstore. Finances were thin with Jonas on long-term disability. "Do me a favor and don't tell anyone, okay? You know how the family is. No one needs to get all worried about me. It's nothing a little chocolate won't cure."

She knew how *that* felt. She slipped the plates on the table and took one of the chairs across from her sister. It was nice; she loved Danielle's home. There were pictures on the walls and toys clustered in the corners and love that filled each room as unmistakable as air.

This is what she'd always wanted for herself. A stable marriage. A warm, loving home. A couple of kids to look after. She'd always just wanted to be a mom. Nothing else. She'd gone to college because her parents had expected it and her grandmother had been so proud of her.

But she'd had a hard time deciding on what to really do with her life. All of her friends seemed to know—they were biology majors, business majors, psych majors. It seemed everyone was so focused, except for her. Now she was through with a graduate degree and she still felt as if she were wandering through life.

Letting Chris go had meant letting go of her dreams. It had been the right thing to do. Absolutely. But just because she'd given her worries and her wishes up to God didn't mean she now knew what to do with her life in the meantime. Her future was one blank slate. She was afraid that she would spend too many years alone, wishing for what she did not have. Worse, she didn't know what to do with her life now, without those dreams.

"You look pretty serious," Danielle said around a bite of pie. "Want to talk about it?"

Yes. No. Too personal. Rebecca took a bit of creamy pie so she didn't have to answer. She wanted to tell Dani about meeting Chad, but if she did, then her sister would so get the wrong idea. Best to keep quiet. It was strange how just thinking about him, about how calm and steady he seemed and how kind his eyes, made her feel better.

Well, maybe he was one of the good guys, she thought, and how nice would that be? It was always helpful to have a decent, nice guy living next door. He'd been a definite knight in shining armor. You never know, she might need that again sometime. Or, better yet, she might be able to return the favor.

She took a sip of milk. "I so don't want to talk about my problems. Tell me how your evening went."

"It was wonderful." Danielle lit up. "Jonas and I had the best time. We went to the museum and looked at dinosaurs."

"Didn't you two take the kids there about a month ago?"

"Yes. And the kids got to see everything

while Jonas and I were watching the kids." Dani laughed happily. "Jonas remembered that every time I wanted to stop and look at something, Madison had a tantrum, bless her. She was simply so excited by the displays and the people. Oh, and she had been wearing her newest mermaid princess outfit. I had my hands full trying to keep up with her *and* keeping her in a good mood."

"So Jonas took you back on a date night." Rebecca couldn't help sighing. Jonas was definitely one of the good guys, too. See, in the long run, the women in her family had a good history of finding the right kind of men, the kind you could count on. Maybe she wouldn't always have to have a No Man policy. Maybe one day far down the road, when her heart was ready to trust again, God would find someone for her. She had to hope that she wasn't marked by her early years, or the painful, bad relationship with Chris.

Have faith, she told herself and took another bite of pie. The chocolate had helped. By the time she pulled into her driveway, she was totally feeling better.

There was a small shadow sitting on her lit front porch. She squinted into the twilight shadows and stopped the car. Why, it looked as if someone had laid a stick in front of her door. No, not a stick. She left the engine idling and stepped into the warm evening winds. A dowel.

A handwritten note was taped to it, bold script on a ripped piece of notebook paper. *To keep you safe and sound.*

She grimaced inwardly. How was she going to keep from liking him now? Chad Lawson was definitely one of the good guys.

It was morning, and Chad had a long list of things to get done for the day. He pondered that list as he folded the top of the cereal box and stuck it in the cupboard. Sure, he had practical things to get done, like showing up for the first day of his new job on time. Run a few errands on the way home from work. But he had one less-than-practical item on that list, and that was to find out more about his lovely neighbor, Rebecca McKaslin.

Ephraim would know. Chad grabbed the carton out of the fridge. Whatever he did, he had to bring her up casually, otherwise his esteemed roommate would leap to conclusions—premature ones. He poured milk over his breakfast cereal. He had learned to be cautious in relationships. It was best to start off slow. Whatever he did, he had to act as though gorgeous, nice-looking Rebecca was no big deal.

He was just curious. That was all. Nothing wrong with that, right? He closed the milk's top and returned it to the refrigerator, not quite sure what he was feeling. Definite curiosity, he decided as he shut the door and went digging through the nearest drawer for a spoon—he was in luck. There was one clean one left.

He shoveled cereal into his mouth, leaning with his back against the counter. Rebecca. What would she think about him if she knew his truths? Would she be understanding? Or would she do her best to avoid him?

The shame of his past mistakes still stung, and it was a harsh sting. There was nothing he could do about that. The past couldn't be changed—not even God could manage that. All Chad could do was his best with today. To keep making the right choices, which he'd been doing just fine for a long time, now. Living the right way was a lifelong commitment, one he took seriously.

What were the chances that a nice, great girl would see that?

He feared he already knew. Probably close

to zilch. He had to try anyway. Asking a few questions wouldn't hurt, right? And he was only curious, that was all. At least, that was his story and he was sticking to it. "Hey, Ephraim."

"Yo." Ephraim looked up from his morning newspaper. Sunlight streamed through the window onto the secondhand dinette set and winked off his nearly empty glass of orange juice. "You need directions to the church?"

"Nope. I swung by there last night." This morning was the start of his new job—volunteer all the way—and that's what he ought to be thinking about. But was he?

Nope. Not a chance. Chad chewed and swallowed. How did he best go about sounding casual? "I met the girl next door."

"Oh, Elle?"

Whoever Elle was, she made Ephraim jerk up from his paper. Interesting. "Nope. Must be the neighbor on the other side."

"Oh, sure. Rebecca." Ephraim's attention went back to the business section. "She moved in a few months ago. I think she's renting the place from her sister. That's about all I know. She's a graduate student, in, ah…can't remember what she told me. English, maybe?

"Why, you interested?" Ephraim turned the page with a newspapery crinkle.

Chad shrugged. Since he valued honesty, silence was the best policy. He polished off his cereal, slurped the dregs of the milk and loaded the bowl and spoon into the dishwasher. Just in time, too, judging by the clock. "I'm outta here."

"Want to swing by for tacos tonight?" Ephraim's attention hadn't returned to his paper. "I highly recommend Mr. Paco's Tacos for their nachos."

"See you there around five?" Chad grabbed his keys from the counter. His sneakers squeaked on the linoleum as he headed to the door.

"She's got a boyfriend." Ephraim's words brought him to a screeching halt.

"A boyfriend?" Chad pounded back into the kitchen. Hadn't Rebecca said she didn't have one? He distinctly remembered it.

"Or, at least she had one."

Yep, that was it. He had to remind himself to act casual. "She might have mentioned that."

"The guy wasn't so nice. Now I remember." Ephraim folded up his newspaper, as if he were planning to take it to work with him. "There was an incident a while back. Her big brother—and I'm talking this guy is big—came and hauled the boyfriend out into the parking lot and held him until the cops came."

"You mean, like he tried to hurt her?"

"I don't know. Maybe. It was a bad scene. It's too bad, too, because she's a nice girl. A great neighbor. Quiet, and I hardly ever see her."

All bonuses to quiet, bookish Ephraim. Chad's guts tightened up. He got a bad feeling, and he didn't like it. He loathed guys who thought it was okay to control women. Sure, he knew what it was like to make a mistake, but he'd been fifteen at the time and he had been hurt the most. Not that that was justification—he'd learned his lesson, he'd paid for his crime and he was a different man now. "She wasn't hurt, was she?"

"No, I would have remembered that." Ephraim stood and lifted his briefcase from the floor, where it leaned against the wall already packed for the workday. "She didn't deserve that. No one is nicer. My car was in the shop a while back and she let me ride with her to church and even dropped me off at work and school for a few days."

That sounded like his impression of her. Chad juggled the keys in his hand, considering. He didn't dare say more. It was best to go slow on this, get to know her more, figure out if he had a chance at all with her first. He'd had a few hard rejections over the past three years, so it wasn't as if he were going to ask her out or anything. Maybe it was worth getting up his courage to get to know her. He'd pray on it.

Not that he wanted Ephraim, or anyone to know how he felt about things. He headed to the door. "I'll see ya tonight."

"Sure."

When the garage door chugged open, he was greeted with rain falling from a slate sky. Not the best weather for day camp. As he navigated the short distance to the gray stone church on a pleasant tree-lined street, he sure hoped Pastor Marin had a lot of indoor activities planned or his first day as a counselor would be a challenge. Not that he minded challenges, he thought as he pulled into the lot and into the first available space he came to.

Well, this was it. Rain dappled him as he locked up. The doors to one of the auxiliary buildings behind the church were opened wide to welcome the day campers in out of the weather. He caught sight of two women standing beneath the awning, with clip-boards in hand.

One of them, squinting at him in surprise, was his gorgeous next-door neighbor, Rebecca McKaslin.

Chapter Three

Rebecca couldn't believe her eyes. Chad Lawson strode through the gray sheets of rain in the parking lot like a hero through the mist. He seemed untouched by the downpour and unruffled by the wind. Something about him made him appear extraordinary. Simply from seeing him, from having him near, the stress of the morning slid from her shoulders like rain from the roof.

No one, except her family members, had ever made her feel so calm.

Marin, the church's youth pastor, leaned close, so her voice wouldn't carry. "Here's someone I want you to meet, now that you're a free and single woman."

Uh-oh. "Why does everyone think I need to start dating?"

"Because you deserve a great guy to love you, that's why. And speaking of one—"

Rebecca rolled her eyes. Good grief. Marin's newlywed happiness had sadly affected her brain. She loved her pastor, but Marin was looking at relationships through rose-colored glasses. And why wouldn't she? She was blissfully happy. All it took was one look to see it.

Good for her, right? Rebecca firmly denied any wistful feelings. Some people were just especially blessed in the love department. How could they understand someone who wasn't?

Visions of Marin's future matchmaking efforts flashed before Rebecca's eyes. Time to do damage control before that could possibly happen. She had to be clear, firm and assertive. "I'm not interested."

"That sounds like a snap decision to me. Maybe you want to think about it." Marin looked so sure about that.

And why wouldn't she be? Any single woman in her right mind would want to think about Chad Lawson. And wasn't that just the problem? She had a No Man policy. It was safer. It was smarter. "I refuse to think about it."

"You never know, he could be the right man for you."

"Yeah, but more likely he isn't. No matter how great he is, because that's my luck." Rebecca rolled her eyes. Just what she needed, her pastor, who was also one of her sister's best friends trying to set her up. "I'm on a vacation from romance of any kind."

"A vacation? I've never heard of such a thing."

"Like you didn't date for a long time?"

"Yeah, well it was different for me. I wasn't on vacation as much as I couldn't catch anyone. Until my Jeremy came along, of course. Just because you split up with Chris and it didn't end well, that doesn't mean you should rule out dating forever and ever—"

"And *this* coming from the woman who dubbed the different phases of dating, one of them being, the doom phase."

"That was before I met Jeremy."

"Excuses, excuses. Believe me, I'm sure about this. Now he's coming closer, so—" Rebecca didn't know how to say it kindly. "No more romance talk. We've got kids coming in a few minutes."

"Sure. Fine. I can take a hint." Marin was smiling a little too widely to be believable.

What was she going to do with everyone? What did she have to do to convince them that she really was fine? Well, as fine as she could be?

Rebecca focused on her clipboard, aware of the slight slap of Chad's steps coming closer. Marin meant well, sure, but she had forgotten what it was like to be single and wish things were different. To wish you, yourself, were different.

She managed what she hoped was a bright welcome. "Chad. I'm pretty shocked to see you bright and early on a Monday morning. You're not a member, are you?"

"I've been here a couple of times when I was visiting my aunt and uncle. They attend the earliest service. I could barely hold my eyes open."

"I try to avoid that one if I can or I'm constantly yawning, no matter how hard I try not to." There she went, yakking on with him again. He was incredibly easy to talk to. "If you're looking for Pastor Michaels, you've just missed him. He left for a meeting."

"No, I'm where I'm supposed to be. Hi, Marin. I'm here on time, reporting for duty."

For duty? The clipboard slipped from her hands and hit the concrete with a stunned clatter. How embarrassing. She knelt to retrieve it but Chad was already there, rescuing it with capable-looking hands. Now, why did she notice something like that?

"Here you go." His smile was genuine. There was that sense of calm again, a steady light in his dark blue eyes. "Are you one of the volunteers, too?"

"No, they actually pay me to have fun with the kids all day." She took the clipboard he offered her. "Thanks. Again."

"No problem."

Why were her knees shaky when she rose? That was a good question. Rebecca straightened the pen, still clipped to the board, needing to look at something other than Chad. She could feel his gaze on her like damp on the wind. Surely he was just surprised to see her, that was all.

Marin was grinning ear to ear. "Since it seems that you two know each other, Chad, take this clipboard and help check in the kids when they start arriving. I'm going to leave you in Rebecca's able hands."

"I don't know about able." Rebecca shook her head. That Marin, she was always so optimistic and complimentary. Chad was so going to get the wrong idea. "I'm lucky you guys put up with me."

Marin chuckled as she walked away.

"Don't listen to her, Chad. She's invaluable around here."

Rebecca rolled her eyes. "Marin is the invaluable one. I'm just hard to get rid of."

"So, have they tried and you just wouldn't leave?" Chad winked at her.

Charming, absolutely charming and she really should not be noticing that. "I've been here every summer since I was fifteen. I started volunteering in the church's day care and it worked into this."

"You've been here ever since? That's some serious commitment. They must really like you."

"I'm the one who really likes it here. The kids are great." She really was surprised how she was just herself around him. It was refreshing. Oh, the dowel. She'd forgotten to thank him. "I found the dowel on my porch. I really appreciate it."

"No problem. I had to stop by the hardware store anyway to pick up a few things." He gave a humble shoulder shrug. "It was no trouble."

"It was still very thoughtful." Rebecca couldn't believe it. Chad Lawson just kept seeming nicer and nicer. "How about you? Why are you here?"

"Why not? My aunt told me about all the

programs here and I thought I would get involved. I'm planning on going to seminary after I finish at the university."

"Montana State? I go there. What are you studying?"

"I'm transferring there. I'm majoring in both religion and psychology. I hope to have a job like Marin's one day. What's your major?"

Here's where it got tough. It was the big question everyone wanted to know. She glanced up to see if any kids were running up to interrupt—and rescue her—yet, but no, there was nothing but the steady patter of the rain. "I just finished my master's degree in English and I'm currently debating going back for my Ph.D."

"Wow. That's great. What kind of job are you going to get with that?"

Yep, there it was. The million-dollar question. "No idea. I just like going to school."

At least that made him smile, and she got to see his friendly, handsome grin again. The sight was enough to make her smile. While talking with him, it was easy to forget how the big plans she had for her life weren't working out the way she thought. God seemed to be leading her in another direction entirely, but where, exactly? "I've never been interested in having a big career."

"You never wanted to grow up and be anything?"

She studied him. It wasn't as if there was anything to lose by telling him the stark truth. "I wanted to be a stay-at-home mom. Maybe that's not politically correct these days, or easy in this economy, but I just loved growing up the way I did. I wanted to be like my mom. To just be happy spending my time taking care of the people I love."

And before he could panic, thinking she was looking for a man to marry and support her, as Chris had finally accused her, she went right on with the truth. "I'm starting to see that's not going to happen for me. That's why I might keep going on with school. I have to believe the good Lord knows where I'm going. Although that sounds easier than it is."

"I know, believe me." Chad resonated kindness. Still masculine and strong, calm and reassuring, but there was a goodness to him. He was more than nice; he was empathetic and mature. "That's faith. To keep putting one foot in front of the other when it feels like you're in the pitch dark, trusting the Lord to guide you in the right direction."

That was it exactly. "You sound as if you're speaking from personal experience."

"I am."

"I don't mean to pry, but did it work out all right for you, walking in the dark and trusting?"

"So far so good. I'll let you know when I get where God is leading me."

"It's to a very good place, I'm sure."

"I am, too." He smiled. He was seeing more in her by the minute. She was grounded and faithful and real.

Before he could ask her anything more, a red minivan pulled to a stop at the curb. The side door slid open and two grade-school-aged kids leaped out, backpacks in hand. They shouted goodbye to their mom behind the wheel, who waited, windshield wipers flapping as the girl and boy splashed their way up the walkway.

Looked as though the workday had started.

Talk about a busy day. With so many kids split up into age-appropriate activities, it was a mystery to him how he kept seeing Rebecca all through the morning.

Not that either of them had a single second to do more than say hi—he was with the older boys and she was with the older girls—but it was nice seeing a friendly face. Other than Ephraim and his aunt and uncle, he didn't know anyone else in all of Bozeman, unless it was Marin, whom he'd met when he'd signed up as a volunteer. So at noontime, when he spotted Rebecca sitting at a table in the dining area with her lunch spread before her, he headed straight for her, tray and all.

"Mind if I sit with you?"

She startled, turning to look at him over her shoulder with her wide honest eyes. The morning of activities had tangled her long locks of brown hair and she seemed glad to see him. "Are you run ragged yet?"

"Yep. I'm beat and the day's half-over." He plopped his plate on the table, keeping an eye on the tableful of twelve-year-olds he was in charge of. The boys were snarfing up pizza and slurping down lemonade as if they were refilling their tanks, recharging for the rest of the afternoon.

Joy. He slid onto the bench near to her and took the time to bow his head for a quick grace. He looked up to find her watching him and waiting for him to finish what he'd been saying. "I'm not sure I can make it through the rest of the day. I'm short on stamina."

"You? Hardly. You look like the type who

is in great cardiovascular health, unlike me who avoids the gym with a passion."

He blinked. Wow. He had just discovered that it was impossible to think *and* look into her pretty eyes at the same time. He did his best to keep his thoughts from scrambling. "You don't like sports?"

"Sure. It's *exercising* I don't like. Treadmills. Weight machines and reps."

"I like the discipline of it."

"Oh, you're one of *those.*" She studied him over the rim of her cup. "I'm surprised you're eating pizza and not soybeans or something."

He caught the amused sparkle in her eyes. "I'm not a total health nut. I used to be, but I missed the pizza. And Popsicle treats. Maybe I should have stuck with the health food and I would have more stamina. Those kids have worn me out."

"Marin should have warned you. You'll get used to it. You look like you're enjoying your first day here."

"I'm having a blast, but I'm feeling my age."

That made her chuckle. "You can't be any older than I am."

"Sure, but those kids are putting me to shame. I'm twenty-four, by the way."

"You're a year older than I am."

Here it came. He might as well say it before she—who had completed a master's program—did. "You're doing the math, aren't you, and wondering why I'm still working for my bachelor's."

"Maybe a little."

"I was a slow starter."

"I doubt that. I saw you playing basketball with the kids. You moved pretty fast."

She saw that? Cool. He took that as a sign. "Sure, when it comes to b-ball. But other things have taken me a little longer to get right."

"I know how that is." She smiled again, and the sweetness just beamed around her like sunlight. She leaned a little closer to him, as if interested in his answer. "Did you have a hard time deciding what to do with your life, too?"

"For a long time." Now would be the right time to be totally honest, to just come clean. He opened his mouth to tell the truth, but the words lodged somewhere deep in his chest, near his heart.

If she knew what he'd done and who he used to be, what would she think? Would she scoot away from him? Try to avoid him the next time she saw him? Would the friendliness in her luminous eyes fade forever, because she saw him differently?

He couldn't say the words. He didn't know if he was afraid to, or if they were just stuck between his ribs and wouldn't budge.

"What's so hard," she said quietly, "is when you think you know where you're going, but life throws you a serious roadblock."

"Been there." Again, he thought about his life before he'd been saved. About the path he'd been on. Thank God for roadblocks. He took a bite of pizza. "I used to have things all figured out. When I was fifteen, thought I knew it all and believe me, that wasn't a good thing. I was making tons of poor choices."

"Who doesn't when we're teenagers?" She took another sip of lemonade and put the cup down thoughtfully.

"You? Make mistakes? I don't believe it."

"Now you're being too kind." She couldn't look at him, but glanced at the table of twelve-year-old girls chattering together or talking on their phones. "I've made so many mistakes, mostly because I couldn't see with my own eyes what was wrong. Even when I was warned."

Chad wondered about what Ephraim said this morning, about Rebecca's former boyfriend. Sympathy tugged at his heart. "That was my problem, too. I had friends telling me that what I was doing was going to catch up with me. That I was hanging with some other kids I didn't think were so bad. I didn't listen."

"I understand. I've been there. I just couldn't see." She shrugged, jostling her long locks of hair, looking sad.

So sad. He couldn't help but be affected. He wished he knew her well enough to know what to do to comfort her. It wasn't right that she'd been hurt by a bad relationship, although he knew, too, what that was like. "Been there. I was seeing this girl, I thought she was fun and different from the kind of sheltered life I led."

"It was a bad relationship for you?" Her hand stilled, her piece of cheese pizza an inch above the plate. "Did you know it at the time?"

"Maybe there was that little voice inside me—you know the one—it was telling me to listen. It's tough to admit, but I just didn't want to."

"Did she break your heart?"

"No, she bruised it pretty bad, though. It was my life she broke." Again, there was the truth right there, but it wouldn't roll off his tongue. Maybe talking about the past just hurt too much. "Nothing was the same after that, and not in a good way."

"I'm sorry you had to go through that." Empathy made her more beautiful. It was easy to see that Rebecca McKaslin had a good heart. She set her half-finished piece of pizza back on her plate. "After you two had broken up, did you take time off from dating for a while?"

"You might say that. It was a long time until I had my life in order before I even tried dating again. That didn't go well."

"I'm sorry to hear that. See, it was different for me. I didn't know the Chris everyone else did." If only she was able to forget the year she'd met him. They'd been high school sweethearts. She'd gotten numb about a lot of things concerning the breakup, but it hurt to remember. It hurt to look back.

She'd made too many mistakes. Mistakes she regretted. "I was seventeen when the coolest guy in high school asked me to accompany him to one of his church functions. He went to a church across town, and when I learned he was a Christian, too, I was so thrilled. He was the captain of both the football and the baseball teams. He went to state three times."

"Sounds like a guy who had everything going for him."

She nodded. Chris had been just *every-thing* wonderful in her eyes. "He was fun and funny and he just seemed to take over my quiet life. It was like the sun came out one day when it had never shone before."

Chad watched her, nodding slowly, as if he were starting to see.

Why she went on, she couldn't say. She was a private person. She didn't even talk about this stuff with her sisters. Maybe it was Chad's dependable goodness. Maybe it was because she'd kept this bottled up for so long. "Sure, Chris had problems, but who doesn't? Nobody's perfect. He swept me off my feet and fell in love with me, and that was an answered prayer. It was all I ever dreamed of."

"Sounds like you still care about this guy."

"No. Yes. Not in the way that you think. Things didn't go…well in the end. And that pretty much ended it for me. But that doesn't mean that it's easy. The hurt is all tangled up with the good stuff *and* the bad stuff." She squeezed her eyes shut, as if looking in instead of out. "Love is complicated. When it ends, it's even more so."

She was a soft touch with a marshmallow center. He could just see how she must have felt. It would be easy to judge, easy to measure out what had happened in black-and-white. But he'd learned the hard way that life wasn't like that, that she was right. Everyone had problems, most people did their best, and when relationships didn't work out, the ending of them hurt like nothing else.

He could see how affable she was. Hers was a goodness that he would guess didn't come and go, but remained even when the going got tough. She was no holiday Christian, and she was no fair-weather friend, either. It was his guess that she had a big, forgiving heart.

When she opened her eyes, she gave another shoulder shrug. "My sisters tell me that's part of healing and moving on. But this love thing is painful when it ends."

"It can be. I think that depends on the two people involved."

She nodded, as if thinking that over. "I guess."

"So this guy, he's the one you were hoping to marry." When she nodded once, he could see more of what she wasn't saying. She had been deeply in love with him. She had wanted a future with him. That had to really have hurt her, especially remembering what Ephraim had said. "There went your dreams and life plan with him."

"Not exactly. That makes me sound as if everything hinged on him. I was just hoping, is all." It wasn't sadness on her face so much as regret. She squared her shoulders, and that regret vanished. "And now I'm on a path I didn't expect to have to turn onto."

"Maybe it's a better one."

"Maybe." She smiled at him, truly smiled.

Just at that second his heart clicked, and he was in like with her. How about that?

Chapter Four

Rebecca hadn't taken two steps out the back door toward the parking lot when her cell phone rang. She was relieved it was one of her sisters calling. "Hello?"

"Hey there." It was Lauren. Together, they were the closest in age and the youngest of the family. "Are you off work?"

"Yep." What she was doing first, though, was scanning the parking lot for signs of Chad. She saw several other coworkers, whom she waved to as she headed toward her Honda parked in the shade of a giant maple tree, but she didn't see him. Bummer. "How about you? Did Spence spring you from the joint yet?"

"Our big brother is one formidable boss." Lauren said the words kindly, with warmth.

"Say no more, Lauren. I completely understand. It sounds like it was a tough day at the ranch." The ranch, meaning the bookstore where Lauren was working until she found a job in her field.

"You know it." Lauren had recently finished her degree in business in California and had come home to stay. "Plus, with the reconstruction going on next door, all I did was listen to hammers banging and drills whizzing all day long. Want to meet for a quick bite? Or a slow bite. I really don't care which."

"Sure, but no pizza." She angled through the lot. "I'm pizza-ed out."

"I need comfort food. Wait, I need Mexi-Fries."

"Then there's only one place to go. Mr. Paco's Tacos."

"Sounds perfect. I'll meet you there in ten minutes?"

"It's a plan." Rebecca clicked off the call. She had five messages waiting. She hit the recent call list—Chris's name and home number were at the top. Those messages were probably from him.

Great. She couldn't ignore him forever, could she? Unless ignoring him was the best solution. Maybe that would make him go away for good. Who knew? She punched her remote and opened her car door. Heat wafted out like poison gas. Not even parking in the shade helped that any.

She eased onto the burning hot seats and turned the engine over. Scorching air breezed out of the vents and she unrolled the windows, waiting for the air-conditioning to cool. Since she was waiting, she might as well look around, right? It wasn't as if she were really watching for Chad—only to find out how he had survived his first day. It was friendly, that was all.

Her phone gave a little chime. It was a text message from Danielle. She shaded the screen with her hand to read it.

Help!! Can U run errand? Call Kath.

Their oldest sister, the one on bed rest, must need something. She would call and find out. Yes, she typed on the tiny keys. No worries.

Thnx. Dani's answer was almost instantaneous. I owe U.

It was no trouble at all. She was always happy to help. She took one last look around the lot—she wasn't watching for Chad, really—and clicked on her seat belt. Since the air was almost cool now, she zapped up the windows and backed out of her space. She caught sight of a tall, broad-shouldered, blond man standing next to Marin's SUV, talking earnestly with her.

She gave a little honk as she drove by—but it was a cheerful honk. She thought of those voice messages waiting on her phone and her hcart felt heavy. It was nice not to have to worry about liking a guy, or dating or being in a relationship. She zipped out of the lot, looking forward to giving Katherine a call, spending some quality time with Lauren and eating nachos until she burst. Thinking of those five messages on her phone, probably all from Chris, she decided that tonight was going to be a man-free zone.

"Yo." Ephraim nodded a greeting from the drink dispensers where he was filling a large plastic cup with soda. "Dude, we're in luck. It's two-fer taco night."

"Two-fer?"

"Two for the price of one."

"Oh, got it." Growing up the way he did, he didn't have a lot of experience with two-fers. He grinned and got into one of three lines at the order counter. It was a few minutes after five and already the place was packed.

"Order the Mexi-Fries and a side of nachos or you'll be sorry. I spot a booth. Let me grab it while I can."

"Okay." Chad stepped forward in line. He checked out what other people had ordered as they walked away from the counter with their bright blue trays. The food looked fresh and plentiful, and his stomach rumbled. The afternoon had been tough on him. He needed to refuel.

After he'd ordered, paid and filled his cup with root beer, he carried his tray to the booth where Ephraim was reading the paper, waiting for him. He realized he didn't have any salsa. He must have missed the salsa bar entirely. He wove through the tables toward the front and spotted the stand where ten different sauces and various garnishes separated the ordering area from the eating area. Then he spotted someone else—Rebecca McKaslin.

Wow. Talk about coincidence—or divine intervention. She was standing in line getting ready to order, talking to a woman about her same age. They were quietly laughing together, and this was a different side of Rebecca than he had seen before. She was a little brighter, more relaxed, and as sweetly merry as a dream. She flicked her ponytail over her slender shoulder and moved forward in line. The woman she was with came, too, and they ordered together. Probably a sister, he figured, remembering she had mentioned having several.

Yeah, it must be nice to have a close bond like that. He grabbed a couple of small plastic cups and started ladling salsa. Maybe if he'd had a brother he was close to, he would have had someone he really trusted to have kept him on the right path. Someone to do more constructive things with. It must be really great to have a large family, he thought as he spooned green salsa into another cup.

He tried not to watch Rebecca. He wasn't a stalker or anything, but his gaze followed her as she carried the tray away from the counter. She looked around, scanning the crowd for an empty table while her sister took the cups to the drink dispensers. Any moment she was going to see him gawking at her. He couldn't help it apparently, so gathered up the cups and looked up just as she spied him.

"Is this divine intervention or what?" She tossed him a sparkling smile that seemed to light up the room. "Then again, it is two-fer night. Wait until the burrito buffet night. That's worth the crowd to come and partake."

"I'll have to remember that." He didn't know what a burrito buffet was, but he intended to find out. "Do you want to sit with us? We have a booth in the back. There's plenty of room."

"Since there are no available tables, I'll take you up on your offer."

That sounded like an excuse to him. There was an itty-bitty table near the door, but she seemed to be ignoring it. That made him happy enough to joke. "Great. You can even bring your sister along."

"That's mighty generous of you." When she smiled like that, little dimples appeared in her cheeks.

Cute. It was hard not to notice that. He pivoted and balancing the four cups he'd filled, headed down the aisle with her. "As you can see, I survived the first day intact, even if I am stumbling from exhaustion."

"That's an exaggeration. I haven't seen you stumble once."

"Sure, but it feels that way."

"Been there." Rebecca glanced over her shoulder and nodded to her sister. "The first day every summer I come home and crash on the couch. I'm not even sure that I blink as I'm staring into space. So you are way ahead of me."

"Yeah, I might be still up and walking around and blinking, but only just barely."

They reached the table. Ephraim looked up from his paper and instantly started to fold it away. "Hey, Rebecca. Good to see you and Lauren. Hi, Lauren."

"Hi. Oh, I forgot the straws."

"Nope, I grabbed them with the napkins." Rebecca slid the tray on the edge of the table but Lauren beat her into the booth, taking the spot across from Ephraim. They immediately started talking about the Bible study they were both in.

"I brought plenty of salsa," Chad was saying as he sat down, "so we can all share. Or I'll go up and get more if you want."

"This will be good, thanks." She unwrapped the paper on her straw, suddenly feeling a little nervous. Just then her phone began to jingle. She fished it out of the outside pocket on her purse and checked the screen. "Ugh."

"Chris?" Lauren whipped around to look at the screen, too. "How many times has he called today?"

"This will make number six."

"He knows you've been at work. He's just doing this to harass you." Lauren pushed a strand of hair out of her eyes, looking concerned. "I can have Caleb talk to him. It might be a good step to take before you go through with getting a no-contact order."

"He wants the attention." Rebecca turned off the ringer and jammed her phone back into her purse. Across the table, both men were watching her with concern, too. This was not the time and place to discuss something so personal and painful. "It's fine. No worries, really. Who wants to say the grace?"

"Ephraim," Lauren and Chad said almost simultaneously.

Ephraim shrugged. "Sure. No problem. Rebecca, if you have any trouble you know you can call us, right? We're right next door."

"That's right," Chad seconded. "We're a few steps away. One call and we can be there in a second."

"Thanks, but there isn't going to be any trouble. My brother made sure of that." She had a lot of faith in Spence, who had intervened on her behalf before. But it was a comfort to hear she wasn't alone and that she had friends who would stand by her. She clasped her hands and bowed her head.

"Lord, please bless this food and our fellowship as we gather in Your name. Amen."

"Amen." Rebecca opened her eyes and what was the first thing she saw? Chad. He was more handsome every time she saw him. It was hard not to notice the friendly slant of his eyes and the way he radiated honesty, which complemented the strong-shouldered dependable impression he gave.

Not that she was interested, of course, but it was hard not to notice or admire. She unfolded a paper napkin from her tray and spread it on her lap. A man of good quality was rare in this world—okay, not so rare, but not exactly an everyday occurrence, either. Maybe that was simply her past experience talking.

She thought of her older sisters all happily married. Katherine, expecting her first baby. Danielle, with two small children. Ava, starting to talk about starting a family, and Aubrey, who wanted a family, too. Lauren was newly married and blissfully happy. They were all with great guys who loved them deeply and truly.

"Chad, this is my sister Lauren. I'm sorry. I think I forgot to introduce you to her."

"That's all right." He dipped one of his deep-fried Tater Tots into one of the salsa containers. "Lauren, it's good to meet you. You aren't the sister with the little kids, right?"

"Right." Lauren unwrapped her straw and slipped it into her iced tea. Her wedding ring sparkled like the amazing gem it was.

"That's quite a diamond you've got there." He couldn't help noticing. "Lucky man."

"Thanks." She looked at her sister. "Rebecca's the only one who is still single and available."

"And determined to stay that way." Rebecca rolled her eyes. "Don't even go there, Lauren. While she is very supportive of me as always, she is absolutely sure I have made a terrible decision with my No Man policy."

"What's a No Man policy?"

"Oh, it's something our sister Ava started." She stuck her plastic fork into her bucket of Tater Tots and caught one with a dainty little stab.

Ephraim unwrapped his taco. "She's the sister with the bakery, right? We've gone to her place a few times for our church's singles' night."

"That's the one." Rebecca dunked the morsel on her fork into the cup of green salsa.

"She's quite a baker, isn't she? We're proud of her. Anyway, she instituted her No Man policy after she had a string of disaster dates. Ava is prone to disaster, so we were never sure if it was her or sheer bad luck."

"I don't believe in luck. I believe in God." He tried one of his Tater Tots—greasy and potato-y. Not bad. He snatched up another.

"Sure, but tell that to Ava after she tried to escape the guy she was dating and accidentally slammed his hand in the car door. Broke two or three fingers. I forget which." Rebecca studied her Tater Tots as if she expected them to hold some kind of answer. "God was gently nudging Ava along trying to steer her into the direction of the man she ended up with. Her No Man policy didn't last long."

"No, it didn't," Lauren agreed.

"She had a space of a few months between the broken finger guy and Brice, who was the contractor renovating her shop. That's when her strict No Man policy worked very well for her. It was the happiest I had ever seen her."

"Except for now that she's married," Lauren corrected.

"So your No Man policy is your quest to be happier." That meant she wasn't happy with the other guy. He took a note of that.

Maybe it was a smart idea to take notes. "How strict is this policy of yours? I mean, you're here with Ephraim and me. I'm assuming that being friends is okay."

"It's okay. It's the dating that is waaay off-limits, thank you very much."

Although she was smiling, it was the little things that spoke to him. The crease of anxiety in her forehead, the tiny crinkle of unhappiness around her eyes, and the hurt that kept her smile from taking over her whole face.

Some might think that her no-dating stance was a drawback considering that he liked her, but he wanted to take small steps slowly. Considering all he had been through, he was wary, too. The last thing he wanted to do was to get his heart broken. He did not want to find out that his fears had merit after all—that a great, wonderful, gorgeous Christian woman like Rebecca would want nothing to do with him if she really knew him.

His chest felt as if he'd inhaled a hive of bees. He took a sip of soda and felt a little better. "I know what you mean. I haven't dated in a long time."

"Really? You?" She didn't seem to believe it.

"I guess that would mean I've had a No

Woman policy for a while, but I'm thinking about ending it." He took a bite of taco before any more incriminating words could roll right off his tongue.

Ephraim shook his head at that. "Dude, I have never had to bother with a No Woman policy. What I need to change is women's policy against me. Do you think it's the pocket protector?"

"I've told you to lose it." Chad couldn't believe it. The girls across the table were trying not to laugh, but it really was funny. "Do you two think Ephraim needs help?"

"I think he needs more than that." Rebecca had the kindest manner. He had noticed it before, but it blew him away now how she gently turned to his best friend. "Which woman in particular has this No Ephraim policy?"

"Sorry. Can't reveal that." Ephraim grinned. "It's privileged information. Classified, even. I could be court-martialed if I told you."

"Lauren." Rebecca leaned close and gently bumped her sister's shoulder with hers. "What do you think—could it be someone in your guys' Bible study group?"

"Could be. There are a lot of pretty girls there." Lauren bumped her sister back. "I'll take scrupulous notes on Friday and let you know. We'll figure this out, don't you worry."

"Joy." Ephraim scowled as if he were not pleased at all with this development.

Chad wasn't fooled. Ephraim just didn't feel comfortable with his feelings any more than most guys did.

Just as he wasn't comfortable when the attention shifted to him. Both women eyed him as if he were next. "Now, wait a minute. Don't look at me. I'm on a No Dating policy, remember?"

"Yes, but you were considering altering it." Rebecca took her plastic knife and fork in hand and sliced a dainty bite out of her soft-shell chicken taco. Ranch and salsa sauces oozed out right along with the cheese.

"What I am considering is ordering one of those next time." Whew, it looked as though he'd successfully derailed her. "Don't worry. I'm nothing like Ephraim. If you notice, no pocket protector."

"Hey." Ephraim good-naturedly protested as he unwrapped his second taco. "The pocket protector is sensible. I do accounting. I need lots of writing utensils and they always leave marks in my pocket."

"Then it is a worthy accessory," Rebecca

said sincerely, although it made the rest of them laugh. "What? Was that funny? Well, the solution is obvious. Ephraim, wear the pocket protector at work and no place else."

"I'm not sure about that. You never know when you'll need a pen." Ephraim's comment made them all burst out in laughter.

This was great, Chad thought, digging into his taco. Tasty food, good friends and laughter. It was an excellent way to spend the evening. He suspected having Rebecca there made all the difference.

It was well after seven by the time Rebecca pulled into her driveway and hit the remote. While the door chugged open, her phone trilled. A new text message. It was from Lauren.

Any more calls?

No, she typed back. With any luck, Chris had gotten the hint. She grabbed her keys and slung her bag over her shoulder. Birdsong drifted in from the open garage door along with a mellow patch of evening sunshine. The leaves in the trees rustled in the hot breeze as she made her way to the bank of mailboxes across the driveway.

"Great minds think alike," came a familiar baritone behind her. Chad walking down his driveway. "Did your errand go all right?"

"Yep. Katherine's husband is on evening shift covering vacations and her seventeen-year-old stepdaughter is off at Bible camp, so we're all making sure she has what she needs while he's working." She waited for him to catch up. "I'm surprised to see you up and about. You said you were going to go home and collapse."

"I got a second wind. Must have been the food and the company."

"Are you ready for another whirlwind day tomorrow?" She fell in stride with him.

"No, but I want to be. It's a lot of fun."

"I think so, too." She unlocked her box, not at all surprised to see bills and junk mail. "Oh, a postcard from Mom and Dad."

"Are they on vacation?" Chad looked up from rifling through the stack of junk mail and bills.

"They are out exploring the West in their RV."

"Sounds to me as if you have a fun family. Sisters to do things with. Parents who go off and explore."

"I like to think we are a fun group. We

have fun together, anyway. I take it your parents aren't the kind to go off and enjoy their retirement?"

"No. My mother is very busy with her charity and my father isn't retired yet. He's one of those workaholic types."

"My father has a very strong work ethic. I think that's why my brother is the same way. He learned at Dad's knee—" She saw a familiar black sports car out of the corner of her eye. She turned without thinking and there was Chris behind the wheel. She could see him plainly through the rolled-down window.

"Uh-oh." Maybe she was wrong about the calls. Her stomach fell.

"What's uh-oh?" Chad asked. "Do you know that guy?"

"It's Chris." She closed the mailbox. "I didn't think he would show up."

Chad sure was giving Chris a hard look as he climbed out of his car. He squared his shoulders protectively. "I can get rid of him for you."

A confrontation. That's all she envisioned. Loud angry words and roughness. Panic fluttered inside her. "N-no. I don't want trouble."

"It won't be any trouble, believe me." Chad drew himself up, as if ready for a fight. "I'll put him back in his car and that will be that."

The sight of Chris powering toward them seeming ominously angry made her panic intensify. She did not want to be alone with that man. But she didn't want to make this situation much worse than it had to be. And there was a bigger reason, a deeper one that had her taking a step away from Chad, too. She was afraid to lean on another man again. She was afraid to trust. "Chad, no thanks. I can handle this."

"No, I don't think so." He looked determined and protective. If ever there was a man who appeared to stand for what was right, it was Chad.

But hadn't she believed in that before and been wrong? The proof of it was stalking toward her. She took a shaky breath and gathered her courage. No, she would be far better standing on her own two feet. "Chad, I said I can handle this."

"But—" He sounded confused, but didn't move a muscle.

She watched in dread as Chris looked from Chad to her. His perfectly baby-blue eyes hardened.

"Who is this, Rebecca? Just what is going on here?" He fisted his hands.

"I'm Chad Lawson. Good to meet you. I understand you aren't welcome here."

Rebecca sighed. Taking him up on his offer would make things easier. "Thanks, Chad, but I want you to go."

"But—"

"Please." Her stomached tightened into one big knot. He meant well, she knew he did, and she meant well, too. "If you want to help, then please go home."

"Yeah, go home." Chris came to a stop, shoulders braced. "I need to talk to my girlfriend."

"Chris, I'm not your girlfriend. Not anymore. Chad, please."

"Fine." Chad looked angry. His mouth worked, as if he had more to say but wasn't about to say it. His eyes conveyed hurt. "You're sure?"

It was tough seeing his hurt, how much he only meant to help her, and she was rejecting him. But she had to. Couldn't he see that? "I'm sure. Thanks, Chad."

He nodded once, saying nothing more and walked stiffly away, his gait tense and a little too fast.

She had upset him. Air wheezed out of her tight throat. She hadn't meant to sound harsh. She'd only wanted to do the right thing.

"Now I see why you have been ignoring

my calls." Chris straightened his shoulders as if posing, looking as handsome as ever in his polished, captain-of-the-football-team kind of way. "You didn't answer my messages, Becca. I must have left a half dozen of them."

"Lauren listened to them for me and erased them." Rebecca was glad she had her cell phone with her. She steeled her spine and gathered up all the courage she had. She wasn't good with ultimatums, especially with Chris. She wasn't good with uncomfortable situations. But right now she had to be. "I told you I don't want to see you. Please leave or I'm calling my brother."

Chapter Five

"What's so fascinating out the window?"

Chad winced. He hadn't meant to get his roommate's attention. He wasn't ready to tip his hand just yet about his like for Rebecca, especially since he had no idea if Rebecca liked him—or if she would ever amend her No Man policy. He stepped away from squinting through the open aluminum blinds. "I ran into Rebecca when she was getting her mail, too. And guess who drove up? That jerk she was dating."

"That can't be good. She's too nice for someone like that."

"No argument there." Chad turned back to the window. "I just wanted to check and make sure she was okay, since you told me that guy might have gotten physical with her."

"Maybe we should go out there and back her up."

"She said she wanted to handle it alone." He didn't know her well enough to have refused to go. She might have thought he was the one being a jerk. He shook his head. "I thought I would keep an eye on her."

"Good plan." Ephraim joined him at the window. "She doesn't know yet, does she?"

"Know what?"

"That you like her."

How had Ephraim guessed? Chad grimaced. What if Rebecca had guessed, too?

"Dude, you do like her, right?"

"No comment." It seemed the safest answer. He didn't take his gaze from her. She was standing straight and tall, her feet braced, her arms crossed in front of her like a shield. She didn't seem happy. The Chris guy didn't, either.

Suddenly a green new-model pickup roared around the corner and came to a stop in the middle of the street. Two men leaped out. The driver was a big guy.

"That's the brother," Ephraim pointed out. "The other one is Lauren's husband. Caleb's a city cop. If I were that dude, I would be shaking in my sandals."

"Looks to me like he is. Think we outta go out and provide backup."

"They don't need it. Look, he's leaving." Ephraim sounded relieved.

But not as relieved as Chad felt. He watched Rebecca's ex head back to his pricey car. Her brother and the cop walked her toward her condo, out of sight. He let the curtain fall. Ephraim had already wandered off to the TV and was flipping through the on-screen channel guide.

Rebecca hadn't wanted him to hang around. He had to remember that. Everything in him wanted to go next door and make sure she was all right. He was torn between doing what he wanted and what she'd needed him to do.

"She gave you her cell number, right?" Ephraim dropped on the couch. "Text her. Calling might be too intrusive right now. She's with her family."

Another car drove up, and he recognized Lauren's newer-model economy sedan. She wove around the brother's pickup and parked in Rebecca's driveway.

Chad stepped away from the window. The cavalry had arrived. Rebecca McKaslin didn't need him, not one bit. Why that struck him hard, he couldn't say. He just knew that he liked her. He knew without her having to say it, without knocking on the door and seeing the look on her face, that she didn't need him.

So that was that. He dropped into the nearby chair, propped his feet on the battered coffee table and tried to focus on whatever Ephraim was watching.

Now that it was all over, the shaking kicked in. It was all Rebecca could do to hold the teapot and not spill as she poured two cups of steaming lemon chamomile. Her pulse knocked in her ears, drowning out the sounds of Lauren getting settled in the second bedroom. Her sister had announced she was spending that night, end of story.

Rebecca set the pot on the counter. Her hands were still shaking. She hadn't been afraid of Chris, not exactly. She didn't think he had come to threaten her. No, he had come to apologize and try to get back together. He had looked sad tonight, as if he were truly hurting.

I still love you, Rebecca, he said with all sincerity. I've never stopped loving you.

Wasn't that the trouble? She thought of his erratic behavior over the last few years. His moods had been up and down. Sharp and unpredictable. Then she thought about the better times when things had gone really well. He made her feel needed and important to him. She was special. And he had loved her. Her heart gave a little twist.

Love. There was that troublesome word again. She had been blissfully happy and dismally unhappy, felt safe and afraid for her safety, and all because of love.

If this was love, who needed it?

Her cell phone chimed. A text message.

"Is that Chris?" Lauren called from down the hall.

Rebecca picked up the phone she'd left on the table and checked the screen. Seeing Chad's name on her new message list soothed away some of her shakiness.

"No," she called back to her sister and, smiling to herself, opened the message.

How R U?

OK, she sent back and, still smiling, slipped the phone into her pocket. Chad. Her heart warmed remembering how he had wanted to help her. And although she had refused him, he still cared how she was. He was a good guy. She stirred milk and honey into the cups and carried them in to her sister.

Lauren zipped her overnight bag closed and shoved it into the closet out of sight. "There. All settled. That smells like perfection."

"And calming, too." She wanted to keep things light. She wanted to wish Chris away. "Are you sure you want to do this? I told you, I will be just fine."

"I know, but we haven't had a sleepover in a while. It will be fun." Lauren sat on the edge of her twin bed. "This is for the best, you know."

There they were, talking about Chris. Again. Rebecca cradled the cup in both hands. "Yes, but what I want to know is how did you luck out with such a great guy?"

"My Caleb is one of God's great blessings." Lauren shrugged. "I don't know what I did to get him, but I'm deeply grateful."

Rebecca's eyes smarted. She took a small sip of the hot tea. She was glad true love was out there. But tonight it felt as if her chances of finding it were nil. Nada. A big fat zero.

Her phone jingled again. Chad? She set the cup down on the little nightstand. "I'm glad Caleb found you. Do you know what we should be talking about? Katherine's baby shower. Hello."

"It's months away. I have the invitations finished. Ava's making the cake. The caterer's set. The flowers are ordered." Lauren leaned back on the pile of pillows and stretched out, balancing her full cup carefully. "Oh, and did I tell you? William has offered to do all the pictures. To think, an award-winning photographer in our own family."

"It's a blessing Aubrey found him, too." There had been a time when she'd been wistful, glad for her sisters but looking forward to the same blessings herself.

But after tonight, that felt resolved. Okay, she had to silence a tiny bit of longing down deep in her soul, but for the most part she was at peace with her singleness. Thank the Lord she was on her own. She shuddered, thinking of what her future might have been like had she chosen to stay with Chris.

She eased the phone out of her pocket and glanced at the screen. Yep, another note from Chad.

"Is that Ava running late?"

"Ava's coming?" Rebecca rolled her eyes. She should have known Lauren was only the first wave. "No, this is from Chad. He was there when Chris drove up."

"And why didn't he stay?"

"Because I made him go. All I could imagine was Chris getting the wrong idea.

That would only make him harder to handle. This way he knows that no matter what, we're over—if I'm dating or not. He might have actually gotten a clue this time."

"I'm glad Spence and Caleb could help with that."

"Me, too." Rebecca peeked at Chad's message.

Need a Popsicle?

Do I!!! she typed and hit Send.

"And why are you smiling?" Lauren asked.

"Am I smiling?" No, that couldn't be right. There was no way she was smiling since Chris was still weighing heavily on her mind. "It's just the neighbor."

"The neighbor. Hmm. Want to tell me more about how you feel about the neighbor?"

"No." Really. Rebecca took another sip of tea and scooted back on the bed. "After this thing with Chris, do you really think I want to jump right into dating again?"

"What I don't understand is why Chris came by tonight."

"He wanted to get back together."

"Why? Doesn't he get that he messed up? He's history."

"Yes, but he wants to start over."

"And you told him…?"

"That I'm not interested in that. I wish I could go back and have things turn out differently—or I used to." She thought of that night when he'd come over and frightened her. He had been so angry and on the edge of violence. "But after I saw that side of him and realized why he'd been behaving the way he had, up and down, and so difficult, then there was nothing else I could do."

"Sometimes people change on you."

She nodded, unable to say the words. "Dumb me. I should have accepted that Chris grew into someone different than the man I fell in love with, but I stayed in denial. I guess I couldn't see it."

"You're not dumb, Becca. Just good and sweet and wonderful."

"Says you because you have to. You're my sister." Rebecca rolled her eyes. And she loved Lauren for it. Her phone chimed again. She glanced down at Chad's message. Meet U out back. "I'll be just a sec."

"Where are you going? Oh, you're going to see him, right?"

"It's nothing romantic, I promise." Rebecca set her cup on the nightstand and headed toward the door. "I'm sticking to my No Man policy, never you fear."

"I was sort of hoping you wouldn't." Lauren's gentle words followed her out into the hallway.

"Rebecca." Spence blocked her way into the living room, glowering worse than usual. "There's some guy on the patio. Want me to take care of him, too?"

"No, but I appreciate the offer." She didn't let her brother's scowl detour her. The trick to Spence was interpreting him correctly. For instance, he looked formidable and snarling mad. Translation: deeply concerned and too macho to show it. "I can handle this one. Go back to your baseball game."

Caleb glanced up as she passed by the couch. "I could help take care of him, too."

"Enough." Now they were jesting with her. She knelt down to remove the dowel.

"Smart idea," Spence called as he settled back into the chair. "Glad to see you're thinking."

Did she dare tell them that the guy on the patio was the smart one? And then they would want to invite him in, probably befriend him and start speculating about their future. Would they date? Get married?

No way. She mentally rolled her eyes and slid open the door.

"Hi."

Other men might look uncomfortable standing on the patio and holding a box of Popsicle treats, but not Chad. No, he was steady and sure.

"I brought the whole box," he explained. "There ought to be enough for everyone."

He humbled her. He ought to be angry with her, but he wasn't. "I'm sorry I sent you away. I appreciate that you wanted to help."

"I still do, Rebecca. That hasn't changed."

"I just had to do this on my own. I'm alone. I have to get used to that. I have to start solving my problems that way."

"You're not alone. You know that, right?"

"I do." That wasn't what she meant. She trusted God. She trusted her family. But it was hard to see past the way Chris's angry threats had hurt her that night not so long ago. Having a No Man policy was definitely the best idea she'd had in a while. "Thank you for leaving when I asked you to. You listened to me. You actually did."

"Of course I did. I respect you, Rebecca."

"I respect you, too." Her chest felt all knotted up. What was she going to do about

Chad? "Do you want to come in? If you do, I have to warn you. I've got an overprotective big brother and five overprotective older sisters. Most of them are on their way over."

"No, this is your family time. I don't want to interrupt that." Chad took a step toward her, holding out the box, but it looked to her as though he wanted to say something else. Maybe it was the waning evening light. Maybe it was just her wistful heart.

Or maybe it was the fact that she hadn't liked any guy so much so fast in a long time. The last time, well, that had been Chris.

She took the box. "I suppose this means we have to be real friends now."

"That's the deal with a grape Popsicle. It stands for so much more than a summer treat."

"I see. We're in luck. I might have a No Man policy, but I do have a friend clause."

"Then it's my lucky day."

A friend. There was definitely no harm in having another good friend. Perhaps things would be better and easier that way. And if a part of her heart gave a little sigh of disappointment, then that was a part that she refused to listen to. "Well, friend, I'll see you tomorrow at work?"

"You know it." He was already backing

away, moving slow, grinning at her with that confident, sincere way of his that could calm her troubles. "I'm looking forward to it."

"I'm glad. You seem to have a gift with the kids."

"Thanks. That's nice to know. Now I don't have to rethink my life's calling." There were those dimples flashing at her. "You're really good with them, too."

Now he was being complimentary. Charming. "Did you know tomorrow is swimming lessons?"

"I heard something about that. Marin told me to bring a suit and a towel."

"You haven't experienced day camp until you've spent a session in the pool. For your sake, I hope you can swim."

"Like a fish."

"Then maybe you can keep up with me." Now why did she say that?

Chad chuckled. It was a heartening sound, soft and low and rumbling. "Maybe *you* can keep up with *me*. Stay tuned. Tomorrow you and I will rumble. Good night, Rebecca."

"Good night." There she went, smiling again. Didn't that spell trouble? She clutched the box as she forced her feet to turn her around and take her back inside the living room and away from Chad. She pulled the door open and her gaze followed his retreating form as he crossed the common lawn and circled around the stone wall that separated their yards.

She was through with handsome, charming, seemingly perfect guys. And that's the way it had to stay. She gathered up her resolve and closed the door.

Gray skies and the feel of rain chased her down the walkway toward the awaiting church bus. Rebecca hefted the duffel bag higher on her shoulder and hopped up the steps. The door snapped shut behind her.

"Rebecca." Chad's baritone rumbled above the noisy bus full of day campers.

There he was, near the back. Looking dashing in a GrayStone Church Bible camp T-shirt and jeans. He'd saved a seat for her. She was smiling again and she didn't want to think too closely about why. She headed toward him, passing seat after seat full of talking kids, laughing kids, squealing kids. He was an island of calm in the middle of chaos. She dropped into the seat next to him and slipped her bag to the floor. The bus lurched to a rumbling start.

"How did it go with your family last night?" he asked.

"The Popsicle treats were a big hit. Thank you again."

"No problemo. Now we're friends. You know that, right? We're no longer just acquaintances."

"Well, I'm not so sure about that." Why on earth was she jesting with him? She didn't have a single explanation other than she liked the guy. He was fun to be around. "I hardly know anything about you."

"I grew up in Lake Oswego, Oregon, which is near Portland. I was captain of my high school football team."

Mental groan. Not another one. Chris had been one, too. Rebecca shook her head, staring hard at the handle of her duffel bag. It was starting to fray. No surprise, as she had been using it for years. Easier to think about the bag than the man seated beside her. Another football captain type. She definitely had the right idea being leery.

"What?" he asked. "You don't like football?"

"I have nothing against it. Go on. Now I know what, like three thing about you. Wait, four." The bus bounced over the speed bumps, and she bounced on the seat. "Grape is your favorite Popsicle."

He bounced, too, and grinned full-fledged. If she had been thinking about him as a guy to date, then her heart would have went *yikes*. Good thing she wasn't looking at him that way.

"Hold on." He turned toward her in the seat. "You are one big question mark to me. I know you have a big family. You're going to school. You have a No Man policy. I've told you something. Now you tell me something."

"I'm not all that interesting, I assure you."

"Try me."

What was she going to say in answer? Especially since he'd arched one brow so that he looked a little like a blond, wholesome, well-groomed pirate.

Double yikes. Her brain momentarily lost function, like a computer searching for its programming.

"All right, I'll come up with one more thing," he was saying. "I love old movies."

"Me, too."

"Maybe we can catch a showing down at the old renovated theater near campus."

"Uh, you mean as friends, right?" She grabbed the back of the seat in front of her as the bus lurched around a corner.

"Right. Maybe we can bring Ephraim. He likes movies. And why not bring along Lauren and her husband? What do you say?"

"I say that sounds like fun."

"I'm glad you think so. How does Saturday night sound?"

"Doable on my end. I'll check with Lauren."

"And I'll check with Ephraim." He planted his feet as the bus screeched to a stop. "How about we all go out for a bite beforehand?"

"There's a drive-in just across the street from the theater. They've got the best milk shakes."

"Sounds like a perfect plan." The doors had opened and the kids were already standing and vying for space in the aisle. "Looks like we're here. Remember what I told you last night?"

"The challenge. How could I forget?" She swept her bag off the floor and stood in one fluid, graceful motion. Her hair was pulled back in a single ponytail again and wispy locks had escaped to curl around her face. Cute. Very cute.

Friends. It was a good place to start. He grabbed his bag from beneath the seat and followed her out of the bus and into the parking lot at the county swimming pool.

She turned to him, a gust of wind tangling

her curls. She couldn't help joking with him just a little. "Now refresh my memory. What did you say last night?"

"I told you to be ready to rumble."

"And what exactly does that mean?" She fell into stride behind him.

He slung his duffel over his shoulder. "I talked to Marin first thing this morning and found out that we're having a water polo game after the swim lessons. Girls against boys."

"I suppose you think you can win?"

"I'm supremely confident."

She tipped her head back and laughed sweetly. "You know the saying. Pride goes before a fall. I wouldn't be counting on a victory if I were you."

"Now who's being overly confident?" He kept an eye on the kids. Everyone was walking in a fairly orderly way into the building. "How about we say the loser cooks the winner dinner tonight."

"Sounds perfect to me. You can cook?"

"No," he quipped. "I'm just really hoping that I win."

Rain began to fall in huge drops from dark clouds, tapping all around him, drenching him in only a few steps. He didn't mind at all because she was at his side. He felt good—

better than he could ever remember feeling—as he held open the door for her and followed her inside.

Chapter Six

Once the hour of swimming lessons were through, Rebecca found herself treading water and unhooking the ropes that had divided the Olympic-size pool into stations for the different classes. She looked up to see Chad cutting smoothly through the blue water to help her.

He tossed her a friendly grin as he stopped on the other side of the rope. "You're a really good swimmer."

"Oh, does that surprise you?" She couldn't help jesting just a little. After all, he had made an assumption that might be a tad erroneous and might work in her favor. What was he going to cook her for dinner? she wondered. Since he didn't have any cooking skills, perhaps he could barbecue. A girl could always hope. "I've been swimming since I was little."

"I guess I didn't think you were the athletic sort." He swiped a shank of wet hair out of his eye. "That will teach me to make assumptions. Luckily, I happen to be a superior swimmer and an excellent water polo player."

"Me, too. Go ahead and talk yourself up, that still isn't going to intimidate me. I intend to lead the girls to a victory." She unhooked the rope and handed it to him. "Why don't you prove your superior swimming skills and take this to the other side of the pool?"

"Now you're mocking me."

"Not me." She backstroked to the next rope.

"Why do I have a feeling of impending doom?"

"No idea. But if I were you, I would be a tad nervous."

"You have super water polo skills you're not telling me about, don't you?"

"Let's just say I'm even better at volleyball." She unhooked the last rope and looked across the rippling water to where Chad was treading water in place, watching her with the strangest look. Not of male superiority or of competition or even of doubt. No, he watched her with respect.

Yep, it was hard not to like the guy. She leaned back and kicked across the pool, taking the end of the rope with her. The buoys attached to it bobbed and dipped in the water. "Friday is volleyball."

"I saw that on the schedule." He kept pace with her although yards of water separated them. He wasn't kidding; he was a strong swimmer. "You surprise me, Rebecca. I wouldn't have pegged you for an athletic girl."

"What does that mean?"

"I have no idea." He chuckled, laughing at himself.

She liked that about him. That he wasn't too serious, and yet he wasn't too superficial, either. He understood about being friends. She was relieved not to have to worry about the whole girlfriend-boyfriend thing. That came with so many pressures and worries. She liked just being herself with him. She hoped he felt the same way.

They were getting nearer to the wall, where kids were milling around taking sides for the two teams and working out positions under the watchful eye of Marin and the other counselors. Rebecca climbed out and plopped onto the side. She wound up the rope, detached it and carried it to the storage closet where one of the pool staff took it from her.

Chad was on her heels. "I suppose this is where we part ways."

"Yes. We're enemies for the next forty-five minutes or so."

"Remember our deal. What are the chances that you will be cooking my favorite meal tonight?"

"I'd put it in the zero percentile." She stepped past him, her feet padding on the wet concrete. How fun was this?

Completely fun. She felt lighter than air as she padded down the deck toward her team. The little kids were clustering at one side of the shallow end, and the older kids in the deep end, which had been divided in half. The pool staff was tying in the goal baskets, a set for each game. The noise as everyone talked was deafening but wonderful.

Rebecca swam into the deep end, feeling great because of her policy. If she hadn't stuck to her word last night, then maybe today would be different. Instead of feeling glad and light, she might well have been worrying about what to do with Chad.

She high-fived a few of her other team members and treaded water near the center line. She hadn't realized how draining her previous relationship had been. This friendship thing was very freeing. She enjoyed being a single, independent woman, thank you very much.

"Captain, it's good to see you're in position." From the deck, Marin gave her a wink. "Do you feel up to taking us to another win?"

"You know it." While the competition was more lighthearted than serious, she wanted to do her part to boost team spirit. "I can taste victory."

She felt a tingle on the back of her neck. She looked across the pool over the heads of the other players who were all milling around in excitement, ready to take their places to where Chad sat on the wall. He might be talking to some of his twelve-year-olds but his gaze was fastened on her. He gave her a salute and slipped into the water. He stroked toward her, moving with ease. He really was a good swimmer. Not that she was worried about losing, of course, but still, the game had just gotten very interesting.

She treaded water as he approached, and she felt all bright and shiny like a perfect summer's day. She really liked that he offered her his hand in a shake—a sign of good sportsmanship. The shake was watery, but represented more. They were friends. She knew they were going to be really good friends as time went on. She liked that idea very much.

Dean, one of the other counselors, held up the ball, and Rebecca prepared herself to spring. She noticed Chad did the same. Since he was watching her instead of the ball, he was slow when Dean's whistle blasted above the pool noise. She lcaped, stretched as far as she could and tipped the ball toward her team. They were off to a promising start.

How had his side lost? Chad marveled about that through the rest of the afternoon and on the drive home. He could be a chauvinist and say that boys didn't lose to girls, but that wasn't like him. Not to mention, it wasn't the issue. He was a good swimmer and a complete athlete. His twelve-year-olds were enthusiastic athletes. The other kids— eleven and ten-year-olds—were no slouches. And Dean, the other counselor on his side, was at MSU on a sports scholarship. All that, and they still lost.

Rebecca and her girls had taken the lead early, lost and recovered it by making the last four goals of the game. He didn't know about the other guys, but he'd really had a workout. He couldn't remember the last time he'd had so much fun. Now he was going to have to figure out what to do about dinner.

He pulled into his driveway and realized that a little red Honda was cruising down the road. He hit the garage remote and by the time he'd parked and dragged his duffel bag out from the backseat, she was idling in her driveway waiting for her door to open.

This was the moment of truth. He gave her a wave and there was no mistaking the grin on her face as she powered down her passenger side window.

"Hey there, stranger." She slid the sunglasses down her nose. "What's for dinner?"

"That's what I'm trying to figure out." He splayed his hands on the sun-warmed car door and peered through the open window at her. "I don't suppose you'll settle for takeout? I could serve it on plates in my kitchen?"

"Not a chance, mister. I'm in the mood for a homemade meal."

"You're torturing me. You know that, right?"

"I do." She sparkled at him like the rarest of gems.

His chest tightened. He sure liked her. Very much. More and more as he spent time with her. The last thing he wanted to do was to disappoint her. "I don't suppose microwaving a frozen dinner counts?"

"There has to be something you can cook. Barbecuing counts."

"Whew. You just made my day. I happen to be a competent barbecuer."

"Good. I'll go in and change and be right over."

"Wait. There is one little problem."

"Problem?" She squinted up at him. "I'm afraid to ask."

"Ephraim's the owner of the barbecue and as far as I know, it's out of propane."

"Hard to barbecue without a heat source." She folded her glasses and slid them into their leather case. "If you're hoping that I will let you off the hook, then you are going to be one disappointed man."

"I don't want off the hook."

"Good." She liked the way he was so sincere in his reassurance. She always knew where she stood with him. "Then you can come over and use mine."

"Great. That's mighty generous of you, Rebecca, seeing as I'm the big loser here."

"You're not a loser from where I'm standing. You play a good game of water polo."

"As do you. I had a lot of fun today."

"Me, too. I'm looking forward to next week's rematch."

"I'll see you in a few." He pushed away from the car.

As she eased into the shade of the garage, why did her heart give a funny little skip? Sure, she was looking forward to spending the evening with him, but as friends only.

She grabbed her gym bag and purse and popped out of the seat. The garage door was motoring down when her cell rang. She juggled her keys, checked the screen and unlocked the inside garage door. "Hi, Spence."

"You okay?" his baritone boomed like furious thunder.

Interpretation: I'm worried about you and don't want to show it, so I'll be extra gruff to hide it. She rolled her eyes. Men. She pushed into the laundry room and dropped her stuff on top of the dryer. "I'm fine. No worries. How are you?"

"Alive."

Interpretation: I'm not telling you anything more. Rebecca rolled her eyes again, locked the door behind her and tumbled into the kitchen.

"Have you heard from him?" Spence barked into her ear.

"No. Chris hasn't called or anything." Sunlight slanted through the blinds, brightening up the oak cabinets and sleek marble counters. She yanked open the refrigerator door and grabbed a can of cherry soda. "Thanks for coming the way you did last night. I shouldn't have bothered you."

"He ought to leave you alone."

Interpretation: I was glad to help. Rebecca knew she wasn't imagining the slight warmth of her brother's tone. Spence was a hard nut to crack, but she had figured out his code long ago. He was a great big brother. "I probably overreacted, but it meant a lot to know that you were there."

"He doesn't get to hurt you, Rebecca. I'm not going to let that happen."

"I love you, too, you know." She so wished Spence would open up, enough so that maybe a really nice woman could see the real Spence McKaslin. But she didn't tell him that—mostly because she didn't want to hear Spence's bitter opinion on most women and the institution of marriage. She was starting to understand why he stayed single. It was so much easier not letting someone close enough to hurt you. If you didn't trust anyone, then you couldn't be shattered when things didn't work out.

The note stuck to a magnet on her refrigerator door caught her eye, one she had written to herself. "Hey, Spence. I don't think I can make it over to the bookstore when Lucy is there tomorrow. Would it be too much trouble to have her sign a copy of her new book for me?"

"Yes."

This time she couldn't tell if he was joking or not. She popped the can's top. "Lucy has a book signing tomorrow. Remember?"

"I try not to pay attention to that woman. Danielle handles the signings. I have a church meeting tomorrow."

What was up with Spence? He sounded even surlier than usual. "Then I guess I'll talk to Danielle."

"You let me know if you have any more trouble with that boy."

"I will." Rebecca wandered into the hallway and bumped down the thermostat. The air conditioner clicked on. "Thanks again, Spence."

"Bye."

Interpretation: You're welcome. The phone disconnected and she ended the call. Spence. She thought of her brother, who was probably still at the bookstore working late as he always did. The only problem was that he wasn't at peace. She prayed that one day he would find happiness with the right someone.

Her phone jangled. It was a text message from Chad.

Hot dogs ok? he'd written.

My fave, she answered back.

In her bedroom, she exchanged her jeans and camp T-shirt for a light summer top and matching walking shorts. She was digging in the back of the closet for her favorite casual sandals when her phone trilled again.

Chips or fries? he asked.

Chips. I have a killer dip, she wrote back.

Fab. Coming over.

She had enough time to reach the patio before he came ambling up with a paper bag half-full. He'd changed, too. He was wearing denim cutoffs and a gray T-shirt. There was something about a man with groceries, she decided. Somehow he looked more handsome as he laid down his load on the bistro table.

"You look prepared." She took a peek into the bag. "I have mustard and mayo, you know. I even have relish."

"So do I, and as I remember I'm the one providing the meal." He plucked a packet of matches from the sack. "I even brought soda, but now I see from what you're drinking that I brought the wrong kind. Black cherry soda. I'll have to remember that in case I lose another competition sometime. Not that I'm planning on it."

"Of course not. But this way you can be prepared for next week's defeat." That made him laugh, and she discovered she liked making him laugh. "I see you brought everything but dessert. I have two grape Popsicle treats left in the freezer."

"Only two? You did end up having a lot of family over. That's nice they cared enough to come."

"I'm very blessed." She began to unpack the bag. "It was a full house last night. I owe you a big thank-you. Everyone wanted a Popsicle."

"Glad I could help out." He lifted the barbecue's lid. "How did it go?"

"Everyone made far too big of a deal over this."

"They care about you. That's easy to see." He knelt to give the propane tank's knob a turn. "You mean a lot to them. It's only right they are protective of you."

"Whose side are you on?" She said the words lightly, but they didn't feel that way. She had not confided in her sisters completely and not even Spence knew the whole truth. That troubled her more than she wanted to admit.

"I'm on your side, Rebecca." Chad struck a match. It flamed to life and he lit the barbecue. "Remember your friendship clause? We're friends now."

"We are." Her throat felt tight and she had to glance away from the man who was so wholesome and upright with the soft rays of the evening sun bronzing him. He had probably never done a single thing wrong in his life. He was the perfect man. The perfect friend. The perfect Christian. Her emotions twisted up tight until she hurt everywhere, especially her conscience.

Chad came her way and dug in the bag for the pack of hot dogs. "Then tell me what's troubling you?"

It was impossible to look into his kind eyes and not be affected. Her throat burned. Deep inside, she felt so lonely with this, with what she had kept from her family. "I haven't talked to anyone about this. I just haven't known how."

"Sure you do. You talk. It's that easy."

Yep, that gentle concern of his sure was dazzling. "It's not that easy, although it should be."

"Try me. I'm here to listen not just cook." He grinned.

"You're winning me over when not one of my sisters could do it. Not even Spence."

"This sounds serious." He put down the package, the barbecue forgotten. There was nothing but her. Just her. His chest filled with emotions too complicated to think about. "Tell me, Rebecca. Trust me as a friend."

"Do you think that failing to tell someone something is the same as a lie? Our faith teaches forgiveness, so when is it right to give someone a second chance regardless of what they have done, and how do you know?"

"Uh—" That was all he could get out before his throat choked up, trapping the air in his lungs. Before his brain stopped working and his conscience took a big ugly bite out of him. He pulled out the nearby chair and dropped into it.

Thank heavens she went on talking.

"There's a lot about Chris that came to light late in our relationship." She swiped at the flyaway curls that had escaped her ponytail to curl about her face. "What he told me was a confidence, and so I didn't spill to my sisters. And then we broke up and I didn't know how to, so much time had gone by, and it was over with. I just didn't want to think about all that pain again."

"I know just how that is." Did he. He fidgeted in the chair, knowing that now was the ideal time to tell her his secrets. The things that were too hard for him to talk about. And yet those words lodged in his throat right along with the lump of his emotions.

"I thought we were over—"

"You aren't going back with him?" he asked with more alarm than he'd intended.

"No. Chris really scared me, and I saw a side of him that he had been trying to hide for a long time." She looked miserable and burdened. "He was using drugs. I didn't know, not until that night he exploded at my apartment."

"He threatened you?"

All the color faded from her face and she nodded. It was easy to see she had gotten a serious scare. That what she had seen that night of the man she had once loved had shaken her.

"He had been keeping his secret from me, and when he admitted it, suddenly everything made sense. All of his puzzling behavior. His up-and-down moods. His old nice self for one day, a tense, angry stranger another. It was a terrible betrayal. He kept that from me while I hung in there and tried to make everything right. When it was impossible, and he knew as much. He knew that I could not be with someone who was doing something that was destructive and wrong on so many levels."

"He knew that he would lose you if you learned the truth?"

She nodded. "He wanted money that night. He apparently was broke and needed cash."

He could see what might have happened. "You had to have been devastated."

"I loved him. I trusted him. I thought we wanted the same things." She looked down at the table, her soft curls falling forward to hide her eyes. Her voice sounded so thin and small and vulnerable. "I don't want to be with someone who deceived me like that. Who would treat himself that way. Who especially would treat me that way. And how do I tell my family now? Chris and I are over. It's in the past and I want to keep it there. Am I wrong?"

"That's hard to say." He couldn't look at her. He felt the hit of her words like individual blows to his conscience. Maybe now was the right time to tell her. She wouldn't want to see him again, but it was better to be honest and straightforward. "I've made my share of mistakes. Some really big whoppers—"

The glass door into her condo slid open and a blond-haired, blue-eyed woman peered out at them with a smile wide enough to take over her entire face. "Oops! My bad. Ignore me. I'll just go back the way I came—"

"Ava." Rebecca popped out of her chair, arms out, and wrapped the woman, clearly one of her sisters, in a warm hug.

His chance to tell her the truth had slipped away. He knew he should feel bad at the relief that spilled through him like cool water, but he didn't. He prayed that this interruption was God's way of giving Rebecca more time to get to know him first, so she would understand. At least, that's what he hoped.

Chapter Seven

"I'm not staying," Ava said as she gave Rebecca one last squeeze and stepped back. "I'm not being nosy, really. I just came by to drop off a box from the bakery. Some pick-me-up chocolate. Never mind me. I let myself in and I can let myself out."

With Ava, nothing was that simple. Rebecca was leery as she smiled at her sister. "Where's the bakery box? If I have to be interrogated by you, then I need to know the chocolate is real."

"Interrogate? I just said I wasn't being nosy, right?" There was no missing the gleam of trouble in Ava's big blue eyes.

Rebecca tossed Chad an apologetic look. "You can see why I didn't want to introduce you to everyone last night. Some of my sisters are the kind you don't want to be seen with in public."

Chad bit his lip, as if to hold back his grin. "Yes, I can see," he said very gravely with a hint of a wry grin. "I would be cautious, too, if I were you. You don't want people getting the wrong opinion of the two of us eating alone like this. It might look as if we are having a date."

"Exactly." Rebecca braced herself for the inevitable fallout. Ava was going to tell everyone about this. "Ava, this is Chad. Chad, Ava. There, now don't you have Brice waiting for you?"

"My husband is working late renovating Gran's mall today, and he's absorbed."

She saw Chad's eyebrow go up. Mall? He was probably wondering if he had heard that correctly. Yes, her grandmother owned the shopping complex where the family bookstore was only one of two-dozen shop spaces. "Would it be all right if Ava stayed for dinner, Chad?"

"Sure." His answer was quick and eager to accommodate. He seemed to be interested in her family, unlike Chris.

See how good this friends clause was working? Her decision not to date for the foreseeable future was one of the best decisions she had ever made. It made tonight as easy as could be.

"I would be intruding," Ava answered. "And besides, I have Rex in the car."

"Rex?" Chad asked, as if he really was interested.

"Our golden retriever. He's like having a T. rex loose in the house. If you don't mind him helping you barbecue, I could bring him in."

"Sounds like fun." Chad, the gentleman that he was, didn't bat one eye. His smile was as genuine as could be. His sincerity unmistakable. "I like dogs. Besides, I want to get to know more about Rebecca. As your sister, you probably have all the good stories."

"You know I do." Ava lit up as if it were Christmas morning. "But I'm totally bummed. I'm going to have to take a rain check. I'm meeting Brice and we're having a late dinner out."

"You can stay and keep us company," Chad offered.

Okay, her opinion of this man was going up by the second. This was not the evening they had been planning, but he didn't seem to mind at all. It was fun being with a spontaneous guy—uh, friend. "C'mon, Ava. Stay. But do me a favor."

"Oh, you're afraid I'm going to tell about when you were little and you used to dress up like a ballerina and everywhere we took you, you were in pink tulle and you walked on tiptoe."

Rebecca rolled her eyes. "Is nothing sacred? I was three years old."

"And how you carried your teddy bear everywhere. It's even in all of Dorrie and Dad's wedding pictures. There was the little cute flower girl, holding her basket of rose petals in one hand with her bear in the crook of her arm."

Chad was chuckling, as if he thought that was cute. Before her big sister could embarrass her any more, Rebecca looped her arm through Ava's and steered her through the doorway. "We'll be back, Chad."

"Great. And don't forget that dip of yours," he called out. "And the chocolate."

"Come with me, Ava." She walked away, wondering why that man always made her laugh. She shut the door to keep in what remained of the air-conditioned air and wove through the living room to the front door.

"Is Chad the Popsicle guy?" Ava asked as if there was more going on than met the eye. "He's cute. He's really sweet on you."

"Sweet on me?" Rebecca opened the door and her face started to burn. Surely that was from the harsh summer sun beating on the front step. "No, that's just your wishful thinking. Chad and I hardly know each other. He just moved in next door."

"Ah, sure. My mistake." Ava didn't sound as if she meant that in the slightest.

That was going to spell big trouble. Rebecca hopped down the steps, already dreading the worst. If her entire family wasn't talking about the Popsicle guy yet, then they would be now.

A friendly woof! shattered the serene evening stillness. Rex was hanging out the driver's side window, his tongue lolling.

"Hi, buddy." She rubbed his floppy ears and soft head. "You understand about my No Man policy, right?"

Rex woofed again, licked her hand as she opened the door for him and tumbled onto the driveway. He loped around her and Ava in one big excited circle and then took off for the porch.

"I have to talk to you about this No Man policy of yours." Ava said as she followed her dog into the house. "In case you haven't noticed, there's a man on your patio."

"No, there's a friend on my patio. It's a fine line."

"Sure, I see that." Ava was grinning ear to ear. "You know I was the one who invented the No Man policy. Remember? I had so many dating disasters, I gave up all hope of ever finding Mr. Right."

"I remember." Here it came. Rebecca rolled her eyes and headed straight to the kitchen. The dog was woofing in the living room, presumably at Chad. "Next you're going to tell me that's when you found Brice."

"I think that's the way it works sometimes. You have to totally completely give up on love ever happening, and that's when it finds you."

Rebecca grabbed a tub of ranch dip from the refrigerator and handed it to her sister. "I wonder how many times I'm going to have to hear this?"

"You're going to hear it from everyone, trust me."

"Oh, I do." She scooped the bakery box off the counter where Ava must have left it. "You got the part where I said Chad was a friend."

"Sure, but you never know."

"What do you mean? I intend to stick to my policy." She knew her family meant well, but her stomach was tightening up into a knot. Love was a painful thing, and she didn't know how to explain her fears. Love hurt, and she had trusted a man who had shaken her to the core. She didn't want to do that again. "I'm happy this way."

"Sure. I can see that." Ava led the way into the living room, where Rex was hopping in place, drooling, his gaze glued to Chad and the barbecue. "Chad's a total twenty on a scale of ten. He's a Mr. Wow."

"Did you hear a thing I just told you?"

"Sure, but I know how this is going to go." Ava seemed so sure of herself as she slid open the door and Rex bolted onto the patio. "Don't worry. I'll tell Chad only the really nice stories so he can't help falling in love with you."

"Lord, help me please." Rebecca looked upward, but all she saw were the green stripes of the awning overhead. She shut the door and caught Chad's smile. He watched her over the grill with a fond hitch to his smile. She saw amusement. As if he was glad for the company.

She was, too.

Chad's side hurt from laughing. He leaned back in his chair and debated if he had enough room for another chocolate muffin.

The tops of the muffins were icing faces decorated to look like funny monsters.

"Go ahead. You only live once," Rebecca smiled over the table at him. "Take the last muffin."

"I'm not sure if I can. They're gi-normous."

Ava stood up from the table. "You two ought to drop by the bakery. Anytime. The dessert is on me, remember that, Chad."

"That's nice of you. Thanks, Ava."

"Sure. A friend of Rebecca is a friend of mine." She whistled and Rex lifted his head from his paws, yawned and climbed to his feet. "I've got to go meet my husband. Becca, I'll talk to you later. Chad, it was good meeting you."

"You, too." He watched the sisters hug goodbye. They seemed tight and at ease with one another.

It was easy to see that he'd been right about her family. They loved Rebecca dearly and were protective of her. As if last night hadn't been proof enough, up close it heartened him to see the attention her older sister paid to her and the endless caring in every word. He understood more about Rebecca now.

He gave the dog a final pat, waved goodbye to Rebecca's sister, but in truth he was hardly aware of the woman leaving. No, it was the woman staying who drew his attention and held it with the same power as gravity keeping his feet on the ground. He liked her maybe a little bit more than he wanted to admit or than he knew was safe.

He got to his feet and began clearing the table. Since he had brought paper plates and plastic utensils, cleanup was as simple as dumping everything back into the bag. He put the lid on the tub of dip, which they had made a serious dent in, and left it on Rebecca's side of the table with the last muffin.

"Well, I have to say I'm impressed, Chad Lawson." Rebecca placed her hands on her hips, watching him with clear approval. "You are not only a decent barbecuer, but you're good with kitchen patrol."

"I'm multitalented. Don't you forget that, even if I don't know how to cook." He rolled up the bag of chips and dropped it in the bag. "I think I'm going to have to learn. I can't keep letting Ephraim cook. He's really bad at it. He's my best friend and all, but there's just no getting around that truth. If I learn from him, I won't be any better."

"There's always those cooking channels on TV."

"Sure, but I don't want to fix something fancy. I need to grill sandwiches. Make a hamburger. Maybe a pot of spaghetti. Simple basic stuff."

"I'm starting to take pity on you. Next thing you know I will be offering to teach you."

"That would be great, Rebecca. When can we start? The sooner the better."

"Most guys wouldn't sound so eager."

"Sure. Most guys don't live with Ephraim. The night I stopped by to see the place and give him my deposit, he was making macaroni and cheese from the box, and he burned it. It was not pleasant."

"All right. I'm convinced." She scooped up the tub of dip. "You did great with the barbecuing. Those hot dogs were nearly the best I have ever tasted."

"Nearly the best? What exactly does that mean? Don't tell me that Chris guy was better at barbecuing."

"No. I meant my brother. Spence is a consummate barbecuer. It's his and Dad's thing. Maybe because they were the only boys in the family so they banded together near the barbecue for moral support, or they are both really talented with tongs. So being compared to him is a high compliment."

"Good. Then I thank you for it." Okay, that was lame, but he didn't want the evening to end, or the conversation. What he wanted was to sit in the waning daylight right next to Rebecca and watch the light change colors. She was that kind of girl.

Yep, he liked her more than he was willing to admit. Didn't that spell trouble? There were so many reasons why he could get his heart broken, but that didn't stop him from taking a step closer to her.

"Tomorrow night is your Bible study night," he found himself saying. "You wouldn't mind if we went together, would you? Since I'm new, and don't know anyone there."

"Yes, because you seem like a really introverted kind of guy." She arched one brow, giving him a stern yet entirely soft glance, the same one that she would give the kids at day camp when they were being a little saucy.

"I might not seem like it, but I'm a really sensitive guy. I might feel awkward and shy."

"You don't strike me as the shy type, but I would hate to think that I didn't help a fellow Christian. So yes, I'll let you tag along."

"Great. I'm looking forward to tomorrow." He couldn't help smiling so wide, it felt as if his face was stretching.

"I'm not. Do you know what Ava is going to read into this? By this time tomorrow, my phone will be ringing constantly with well-meaning sisters wanting to know the scoop about you and me."

"You'll have to explain your friend clause."

"I'm glad you understand." She focused her cinnamon-brown eyes on him, and suddenly she looked vulnerable with her heart exposed. "Relationships are hazardous things. Starting one is like taking a journey you've been looking forward to all your life. It's wondrous and amazing and right, but everything can go wrong in the blink of an eye and it doesn't even have to be your doing. I don't know if I can trust another guy like that, at least not for a long time."

"I understand that. Who you trust is a big deal. You give the wrong someone your trust, and you get hurt. I know." And he did. He thought of his past mistakes and he knew the shame was always going to be there.

"You have never said why you have a No Date policy?" She took a step closer to him. "What happened? Wait, it's none of my business. I didn't mean to pry. I just care about you. You know, as a friend."

She was quick to add that, and she was

kindness itself but that didn't lessen the sting to his heart. He liked her too much. There was no doubt about that.

"No. The truth is I've been through some stuff and didn't want to involve anyone with what was going on. It was complicated. When life was uncomplicated, I couldn't find the right woman." Here was another place he could tell her the whole truth. But could he? He tried. He opened his mouth, determined to say the words and they died in his throat.

"I completely understand." She waved away her own question. "Enough said. What you and I need to do is to focus on the present and move beyond the past. Leave it where it belongs. Deal?"

"Deal." He blinked. He was still trying to work up the nerve to be wholly honest with her and now another opportunity had passed. Now he had another problem: he didn't want the evening to end. Since there was no more reason to stay, he grabbed the bag.

"Thanks for cooking. You are a good sport, Chad."

"An agreement is an agreement. It was my pleasure. Are you up to a rechallenge next week?"

"I'm looking forward to it." She hesitated at the door, seeming happy. No, it was more than that. She radiated goodness and joy.

His chest cinched up tight. Emotion too sweet to name all but lifted him off the ground. It had to be clouds he was walking on as he hiked onto the grass, walking backward so he could keep sight of her as long as possible. "Good night, Rebecca."

"Good night."

They were officially friends now. Eating dinner together. Helping other friends together. Going to church activities together. The sun seemed to shine more brightly when she gave him one last smile before heading inside. He was definitely in a whole lot of like with her.

God willing, he wasn't about to get his heart broken. He crossed the lush green grass and skirted the wooden wall that separated her yard from his. The phone in his pocket buzzed, and he checked the screen.

Dinner tomorrow night? Rebecca had texted.

Something told him he knew what she had in mind. He dropped into one of the plastic chairs on his patio and typed an answer. Is it burrito buffet night?

Her message came back almost immediately. Yes!

Then count me in, he typed.

The sliding door opened behind him. It was Ephraim back from dinner at his parents' with a plastic-covered plate in hand. "Hey, got my laundry done. Mom sent me home with some brownies."

"That was nice of her. How are your folks?"

"The same. What's going on here? I'm gone for a few hours and I come back to find you grinning ear to ear. And texting someone. A young woman, maybe?"

"Maybe. So, do you want to tell me about our neighbor—"

"Rebecca? There's nothing else to tell. You *really* like her, don't you?" Ephraim took the other chair and they stared out at the lawn, the shrubbery and the opposite patio in companionable silence. He unwrapped the plate and wedged it onto the plastic footstool between the chairs that served as a table. "Don't want to tell a lie, huh?"

"Not sure what I can say that won't either be a lie or incriminate me."

"Understandable." Ephraim took a brownie.

"You know how it is. The other morning you mentioned the neighbor on our other side."

It was Ephraim's turn to choose a moment of silence before he answered. "Two college girls live there. Elle and Sydney."

Maybe Ephraim wasn't aware that his voice deepened when he said Elle's name. Chad took a brownie and bit into it. "Elle and Sydney. Are they nice?"

"Yep." Nothing more.

"What's Elle like?"

"I thought you liked Rebecca." Ephraim used a diversionary tactic.

"Ah, but there's a greater question. Does Rebecca like me?" And an even more gigantic one. Would Rebecca understand when he told her the whole truth about his past? Or would she see it as a deception, a secret he had kept hidden from her the same way Chris had done?

His stomach twisted up. He couldn't shake the troubled feeling gathering like a thunderstorm in his chest.

"I think she likes you," Ephraim answered.

"As a friend." That shouldn't depress him, but it did. Chad bit into the moist crumbly brownie and reflected on the day. It had been a great one, and all because of her. Friendship could turn to more. He was going to stay hopeful for that.

"She's probably just a little gun-shy." Ephraim polished off his brownie and helped himself to another. "You just need to show her that you're nothing like that other guy, that's all."

Gun-shy, sure. That he could understand. "D-do you think she will bolt when she learns I've got a record?"

"Hard to say. You won't know until you tell her." Ephraim lowered his voice. "She's a nice girl. I think she might be sympathetic. You were fifteen and going through a hard time."

"That's no excuse. I wish it was, but it's not." Chad took another brownie and thought while he chewed. He'd known exactly what he was doing back then; he had wanted to do something, anything, to escape the pain of his parents' breakup. Stealing a car for a joyride had been sheer escape, that was for sure. And the friends he had been with assured him they did it all the time—no problem, they had never been caught.

God had surely been watching over him that day, otherwise where would his need for recklessness have taken him? Being arrested and paying for the crime he had committed was one of the best things that had ever happened to him, because it changed the direction of his life.

But would Rebecca see that? Would a young woman with the sheltering love of her family, with her wholesome upbringing and her sweet nature, understand that he was more than the sum of his mistakes, that he was not the kind of man who made them a second time?

Only time would tell. That was the hard part.

"I had the best time tonight." Rebecca tucked her cordless phone between her chin and her shoulder and wandered down the hall. An hour hadn't gone by since she and Chad had parted ways and already two of her sisters had called. Danielle had heard from Ava that there was a new man in her life and now here was Katherine calling for the scoop. "It was friendly. That's it. We're friends."

"Friendship can lead to something more." There was a note of happiness and hope in Katherine's gentle voice.

It was the hope that was hard to face. She knew her family wanted the best for her, but right now a relationship was far from the best thing. She wanted peace and safety. "In this case, it can only lead to more friendship."

"That's what I'm saying. That's what Jack and I have. It's the deepest kind of friendship based on love and respect."

That was hard to argue with. There was no way she could say that she wasn't ever interested in that kind of an amazing relationship one day, but not for a really long time. "I've been in a long-term relationship. I've been dating Chris since I was in high school. I want to take a breather."

"Uh-huh. Sure. But remember this, good things happen to good people, and I have a feeling that something really wonderful is going to happen to you when you least expect it."

Rebecca rolled her eyes. "You have been talking to Ava. She says love happens when you least expect it. You are both right, I'm sure, but I don't want love right now. I want to spend some time and figure out my life. I want to enjoy being young and single because one day I hope to be you, Katherine."

Her laughter was soft and merry. "I'm pretty happy. I want this joy for you one day, too, sweetie."

She knew. That was why her sisters' constant nosiness was really the nicest thing. For almost as long as she could remember, she had been surrounded by the people who loved her most. Maybe that was why things didn't work with Chris. She assumed that he would be unconditionally loving and devoted to her, but he wasn't. That's the way she expected love to be. Love had not meant that in his view.

"Now, tell me more about this Chad."

Here it came. Rebecca stepped into her bedroom and grabbed her Bible and her study book from the nightstand. "He belongs to our church, he volunteers at the day camp program, and that's all I'm going to tell you."

"He must be nice if you like him."

"I wouldn't be *friends* with him if he wasn't." She couldn't help laughing. Her sisters. She shook her head. What was she going to do with them? First off, she was going to give thanks for them as soon as she could. "I think it's time we talked about you. How are you doing? Do you need anything?"

"I'm great, although time has never passed so slowly. There's so much to do to get ready for this baby, and I'm sitting here with my feet up."

"That's why you have us, you know. I'm happy to do anything for you."

"I'm fine. Just a little frustrated. I want time

to move faster so this baby will be here safe and sound and Jack and I can dote on him."

"I want that, too." Rebecca heard her cell phone chime in the other room. Chad leaving a message? And why was she hoping so?

"Oh, I've got Aubrey calling in. I'd better take this. I need to get their flight information," Katherine said.

"Okay. Bye." She hung up just in the nick of time because she feared Katherine was going to turn the conversation right back around to Chad.

Her family would come to understand in time when they saw she meant what she said. She had plans that involved keeping her heart safe, thank you very much.

She hung up the phone and headed toward the living room. Her cell was on the coffee table where she'd left it, with a new next message. Okay, she didn't have to read it right away, did she?

She sat down on the couch and set her books on the cushion beside her. It was a lovely room. Katherine had left most of her furniture behind when she married Jack, since his house was fully furnished. Rebecca had always felt comfortable in this place, and now that her own things were here, too, she felt settled. Part of her would always want the dream of a husband, kids and a roomy house for all of them, though for now, she was cozy. She loved this condo, but maybe it was time to start deciding what she wanted besides the dream.

Good friends had to be one of those things, so she reached for her phone.

Thnx for the great evening.

That made her smile. Thnx for the great company.

His answer zipped right back. Looking forward to tomorrow.

Me, too, she typed, smiling all the way down to her soul.

Chapter Eight

"So this is a burrito buffet."

Rebecca grabbed a tray and a plate and took her place in line. "It's build your own. Don't tell me you have never built your own burrito before."

"Can't say as I have. I hadn't realized I was lacking in some important basic skills."

"It's a good thing you're hanging with me." She set the tray on the metal bars and waited her turn to choose a tortilla. "I take it you didn't go out for burritos in Oregon."

"Not like this."

"Oh, so you normally hang out at ritzier places?"

"Yes. My parents tended to drag me to the nicer establishments."

"I'm starting to get a better picture of the

real Chad Lawson." Rebecca grabbed the tongs and lifted a giant-size spinach tortilla and dropped it on her plate. She handed Chad the tongs and noticed his appalled look. "Don't worry. I didn't mean that in a bad way."

"Well, I just don't want you to get the wrong impression."

"What wrong impression?" She scooted her tray down to the choice of meats and ladled spicy chicken into the center of her tortilla. "You're not a bad guy."

"Oh, thanks." He grinned, showing his dimples. "But I've made my share of mistakes. I've told you that."

"Yes, I believe the term you used was whopper." She returned the spoon and reached for a ladleful of black beans. "I'm getting more and more curious about you, mister. I've told you all about my past dating woes and you know about my family. Once again, I don't know enough about you."

"What is it that you specifically want to know?" He spooned beef onto his flour tortilla.

"Why haven't you told me that you come from a privileged background?"

"I'm not too sure about the privileged part. That's a matter of perspective." He pushed his tray next to hers and filled a serving spoon with shredded cheddar. He looked uncomfortable. "My dad owns a software company—it was my grandfather's really."

"A big company or a small company?"

"Try huge."

She pushed her tray down to the garnishes and chose little paper cups of cilantro and salsa. "My grandparents own a lot of commercial land in town. Grandpop has passed on, but Gran is still with us. She's what some people would consider rich. But my family isn't."

"Mine is."

"And you?" Why did she ask that? She hadn't meant to. The words had just popped out. It wasn't any of her business.

"That would be an affirmative." Chad took her tray along with his. "I'll go look for a table. It's really packed in here."

"College kids get a discount," she explained.

They grabbed drinks at the beverage station. She filled the plastic cups and carried them ahead of Chad through the crowd in search of a table. They got lucky. A couple was just leaving and they snagged a booth along the bank of windows, which was relatively private.

It was nice and companionable being with Chad. She felt more relaxed and at ease with him than ever. Surely this was a sign that they really were good friends. If she worried about what her sisters had said about friendship and love, she had to disregard it. For the first time in her life, being with a guy felt right. She and Chad just seemed to click.

As she said grace, she added a silent word of gratitude for Chad's friendship—for it was friendship and nothing more.

"Don't get me wrong," she said as she tore the paper from her straw. "But why are you here instead of some fancy Ivy League school?"

"It's complicated. I wound up missing a year and a half of school. I graduated six months late."

"What happened?"

"Remember those whoppers of mistakes I mentioned? It was one of those."

His eyes darkened when he was sad, she realized. "At every moment of our lives, we get a chance to do what is right. If we choose one thing, then our lives go in one direction. If we choose differently, then it goes in another."

"Exactly. It's called free will." He cut into his burrito and took a bite.

"Yes, and it's tricky. Even when you think you're doing the right thing, it can turn out wrong."

"Yes. I can see you understand that." It meant a lot. He was grateful that she was compassionate. Maybe there was a real chance. It was more than hope, he realized, it was a wish rising up from his soul. "Although I can't believe you have made any whoppers."

"Believe it. One is Chris."

"You loved him." Chad set down his knife and fork. He no longer felt hungry. He had forgotten about everything but the woman in front of him. Not even his worries remained. There was only her sweetness and her beauty. "You're afraid of making the same mistake again."

"Yes." No one—not her other friends and not even her sisters—had understood that. "I don't want to get hurt. Do you think a person is destined to keep making the same kinds of wrong choices? Or do you think that a person can break the patterns of her life?"

"I definitely believe in second chances."

His opinion mattered to her. She felt a little better. "That's what I want to believe."

"It's true. God may have given us free will, but He is the first one to forgive us when we make mistakes." He looked wise, as if he spoke from experience, as he leaned a little closer. His expression was intense but compassionate, too. "Believe me, I know. There is no destiny other than the one God has for you and the one you choose."

He made her feel one hundred times better. The burden she had been carrying on her shoulders over Chris and over the worries of her real father faded away. She took a sip of lemonade. "You are going to make a wonderful pastor."

"I'm glad you think so. I'm not so sure." A little humble and maybe a little self-conscious, he gave her a small shrug before he took another bite of his meal.

She was absolutely beyond a doubt sure that this friendship was one relationship she would never regret.

She led the way down the long corridor to the only open door at the very end of the hall. Voices murmured through the walls of other classes and groups who were meeting, giving her a satisfied feeling. This church and its buildings were some of her favorite places.

"I grew up here," she told Chad in a low voice. "Right across the hall is where I used to have Sunday school when I was itty-bitty."

"It must be something to have roots like you do. Not only with your family, but with your church family right here."

"You didn't grow up in that way?"

"Hardly. My parents aren't disbelievers, but they aren't believers, either. We always attended Christmas Eve and Easter services when I was a kid. I think I would have liked being part of something bigger than myself, even back then. I love Sunday school, and the summer day camp is a blast even as an adult."

"I think so, too." She led the way into the empty classroom. "I would do it year-round if I could. How did you find your faith?"

"One night when I was down, and I mean really down, I felt so alone and it was the most horrible pain. I remembered something far back from one Christmas service. The minister had spoken on a passage and I remembered it. He said nothing is impossible with the Lord. I was out of hope, I was out of luck, and I was terrified. I figured that was a pretty impossible situation and I prayed. That night I gave my life to God and started new."

He stood there in the doorway with his shoulders straight and his baritone rich with sincerity like a perfect face of faithfulness. Her heart fluttered. Yes, it was very hard not to absolutely adore him—in a friendly way, of course.

"I'm glad," she told him. "I'm sorry you

went through such a hard time. Maybe you will tell me about it some time. I'm very glad that you have been led here. I really need someone like you in my life."

"Funny, I feel the exact same way about you." His grin was lopsided, maybe a little sad, as he looked around the room. "Wait, I should have asked this earlier but this isn't a singles' group, is it?"

Rebecca slid her bag onto a table top. "Would you panic if I said yes?"

"I'm debating it." His dimples cut into his cheeks. He was dashing in his black cotton shirt and worn jeans as he scanned the large classroom. "No one's here yet."

"We are, and besides, we're early." She pulled her study book and Bible out of her bag. "We can share, if you want. I was going to drop by the bookstore on my way home. I could pick up another copy for you."

"Why don't I tag along?"

"I wouldn't mind the company." She slipped her bag beneath the table.

"Great." He settled in the chair next to her. "Do you always arrive early?"

"Yes. I don't like to be late. We haven't talked about why you decided to be a youth pastor. That's a serious calling."

"Remember those whopper mistakes I keep mentioning? That's why." There wasn't sadness in his eyes or self-pity, but determination.

Impressive. She shifted in her chair, drawn to him. Yes, she was. Was it a crime? No, so she shouldn't feel troubled by it. "You want to keep others from making mistakes?"

"I know what it's like to have a family torn apart. I know what it's like to go through some painful times and how easy it is to make a wrong decision out of pain or the need to escape it for a while." Chad's sincerity was unmistakable. "I want to be there for other kids and be a guide to help them in a good direction."

"Was that something you just decided to do, or was it a deeper thing?" Rebecca stared down at the worn cover of her Bible. "How did you know?"

"One day it just hit me that I could help others, and use some of those mistakes in my life and turn them into good. It wasn't a decision. More like a sudden knowing. A good fit. I don't know how else to explain it."

"I'm glad for you. You seem sure of your path. I know it's the right one for you."

"You mentioned that you keep taking

classes and hoping the Lord knows where you are going, right?"

"You remembered that?"

"Sure."

"How rare. A man who actually listens." She felt a warm tenderness come to life within her heart, and it wasn't because of him, she thought. It was probably indigestion from eating a second burrito. "I give you high marks, Chad."

"That means a lot. I would rather have your high marks than anyone else's. You're pretty great, Rebecca."

"That's nice of you to say, considering I don't know what I want to do with my life."

"Yes you do. You told me once, remember?"

"I want to take care of the people I love. That isn't exactly a job title."

"You never know. God is leading you somewhere. You should have more faith in Him."

"I do. It's me. I don't have faith in me." She covered her mouth too late to hold back the whole truth.

"I do." He reached over and wrote a chapter and verse on her notebook. Proverbs 16:9.

"Proverbs?" She couldn't recall the exact passage, but she knew she ought to. She flipped open her Bible to Proverbs. Her heart gave a hard thump. *"In his heart a man plans his course, but the Lord determines his steps."*

"Follow your heart," Chad told her, "and God will lead you."

Other people started arriving, and while she greeted old friends and a few new ones and introduced Chad to everyone, his words stuck with her.

He had such a great time, Chad reflected as he followed Rebecca's sporty red car through the sun-washed streets. White thunderheads were building up at the horizon, but they were far away. Nothing could mar the jewel-blue sky and the joy that had burrowed into his heart. Whatever this emotion was, he had never felt it before.

He whipped into a shopping complex's parking lot. It might have been a fine place once in the fifties, judging by the architecture. He rolled his pickup to a stop beside Rebecca's car and climbed out. Corner Christian Bookstore was written across the glass. It was hard to read with the glare of the low slanting sun. They walked beneath a striped awning to the front door.

"Be warned," she told him. "Spence is probably still here. He's always here. He's always in a bad mood whenever there has been a book signing."

"Your brother works here?"

"Remember I told you about my grand-mother? She owns the buildings and the property. The bookstore used to be hers, too, then it was my parents', and now Spence manages it for them."

"I don't suppose you have a trust fund, too?"

"No, do you?" Rebecca shook her head, scattering her soft brown curls. "Wait, don't say it. You have a big trust fund, don't you, and more money than you know what to do with?"

"I live simply. Money doesn't buy happi-ness."

"That's true." She shook her head at him, and he didn't know if that was a good or a bad thing. He only knew that she didn't treat him a bit different as she kept talking. "All I can do is apologize for Spence up front. His bark is much worse than his bite. I'm sorry."

He opened the door and held it for her. "Sorry for what?"

"You'll see. Maybe with any luck he won't be in too terrible of a mood. Remember, he's a good big brother."

Chad stepped one sneaker inside the store

and there was the man he recognized from Rebecca's living room that one evening. Only this time the man seemed even taller and more intimidating. He was wearing an impeccable suit without a single wrinkle and a frown severe enough to scare children, had there been any in the store.

"Spence." Rebecca rushed up to him. "Did you remember about my book?"

"She's still here." He jammed his thumb toward the back of the store. "She was supposed to be done hours ago, but she's still here."

Chad had no idea who they were talking about, but he knew one thing. The brother didn't seem to like him. It was best to make a good first impression, so Chad stuck out his hand. "Good to meet you, sir. I'm Rebecca's neighbor, Chad Lawson. We work together at the church day camp."

Spence grabbed his hand and shook. Hard.

Chad stood his ground and didn't allow himself to wince. "You have a nice bookstore here."

"We try." Spence spit out the words. He did seem like a truly unfriendly fellow. "I've got calls to make."

Chad watched the big man stalk off. He

could have been a soldier on a mission, he moved with that much determination and discipline.

"That went pretty well, considering." Rebecca led the way through the stacks. "I think he likes you."

Okay. It could have gone worse. Chad followed her down the long aisle of Christian fiction to where a blond-haired sunny-looking woman was slipping a handful of books onto a shelf.

"Lucy?" Rebecca called out. "How did the signing go?"

"About ten people showed up, and your brother made the comment that I was taking up space in his bookstore." The woman shook her head, as if she found it all almost funny. "I thought I would annoy him by staying and signing everything of mine you guys had in stock."

"He hates that." Rebecca agreed. "Lucy, this is my friend Chad Lawson. He just met Spence, and it went rather well."

"Yes, I'm sorry, I couldn't help overhearing. It's nice to meet you, Chad. It really was a warm and fuzzy greeting for Spence."

"I heard that," a deep baritone boomed from a few aisles over.

Rebecca giggled. She was endearing, with her brown hair framing her heart-shaped face. She looked at home here, as if she belonged. She loved the people here, he realized. Not just her family, but the customers, too, and this woman with the undefeatable smile.

"I thought you were going to your office," Rebecca called out.

"I was, but I need paperwork from the back room." His footsteps pounded on the carpet growing closer. "How much longer are you going to torture me, Lucy?"

"Sadly I am almost done here. I have signed and stickered the very last book. Thank you for having me, Spence."

"Danielle was the one who wanted you here, not me. Excuse me." He kept going, refusing to look right or left and especially at Lucy.

Interpretation: either he really liked Lucy or he was in a bad mood about something else.

"I signed a book for you," Lucy was saying. "I left it behind the front desk. Spence remembered to ask for one. Hey, I heard all about you. Congratulations. I'm really happy for you."

"Uh, what did you hear?" She winced, her mind spinning. What had her hopeful sisters been saying now?

"That you are on a vacation from romance.

Sometimes that is the best thing to do. I did that once, and developed a really good friendship. It was with the man I eventually got engaged to long ago and almost married. We were friends, and then we were good friends and then it deepened into this rich and beautiful affection."

Was God trying to tell her something? Or was this just coincidence?

"You should never settle for anything less, that's my opinion anyway. But then I'm a romantic." Lucy slipped the last book on the shelf. "Something is bothering me about your name, Chad. I knew a Chad Lawson when I lived in Lake Oswego."

"Y-you're from Oregon?" He took a step back.

"Yes, except the Chad I knew was in his eighties and passed away a few years ago."

"That was my grandfather. I'm named after him."

"He was a fine man. I interviewed him for a book I was writing set during World War II. He had a wonderful sense of humor. I'm glad to know you, Chad. You look like you're a fine man, too."

Rebecca could read the pain on his face easily, but she could sense more clearly the pain in his heart. She didn't know how, but it was as if she knew. This had been difficult for him.

"I can't compare to him, although I would sure like to one day. Maybe when I'm eighty, I'll be half as good a man as he was." Chad straightened his shoulders.

It was simple to see the goodness in him and the strength of character. Maybe that's why she liked him. It struck her then that maybe what she felt was more than like.

She had a crush on her friend. That was a serious violation of her No Man policy. She had to stay a single and independent woman. No crushes were allowed.

Or were they? She considered that question as she waved goodbye to Lucy and helped Chad find the book for their Bible study. That question remained at the back of her mind and in the places in her heart where he had already touched with his kindness, his humor and his understanding.

Yep, she thought as she waited for him at the register, she was in big trouble.

"What did you get?" Chad asked her, leaning over her shoulder to get a look at the two books she'd picked up. "Hey, those are the same book."

"One is for Katherine. I'm going to drop Lucy's new book by her house on my way home. She hasn't been complaining, but I'm sure it has to be hard to stay off her feet all day and night. She's got three more months to go."

"You're a good sister." He said that like a compliment.

"I'm not so good." She blushed. "What is it that you said about your grandfather? That you can't compare?"

"Then I understand that, too." He took his bag, thanked Maggie the cashier and led the way toward the doors. Spence was straightening books on a shelf and gave him one final intimidating stare.

Message received. Be nice to Rebecca. Chad nodded once in answer, because he didn't intend to be anything but nice to her. He held the door. "Look at that sunset."

"It's gorgeous." She stepped out into the rosy hue that had fallen across the world. She seemed to drink in the loveliness, somehow making her more wholesome and perfect in his eyes.

His feelings were sort of like that light, soft and subtle and yet it had the power to change everything.

Chapter Nine

"You and Chad seem to be getting along," Marin commented one morning in the church's multipurpose room. They were setting out watercolors for the younger group. "I hear that you two have been spending a lot of time together."

"Do I have to go through this again?" Laughing, Rebecca shook her head. "Do you know how many calls I got about this? We're friends. How many times do I have to say it?"

"Probably a few hundred more," Marin sympathized. "It was like that with Jeremy and me, too. I had given up all hope and wasn't going to be fooled into trying to date again, and suddenly we were friends. Then suddenly, we were best friends."

"I keep hearing that, too." Really, it was not

a sign from above. "I have a friends-only policy with Chad."

"You wouldn't think about changing it at all, you know, just to see if he's the one?" Marin dug a box of watercolor brushes out of the closet.

"Not even. I'm enjoying being single." That was the truth, but there was more she was still trying to figure out. Now that she could no longer deny having a crush on Chad, did that have to change things? She didn't want anything serious, so did that mean she should take a step back?

"And while I've got you here, let me ask you this." Marin set the box of brushes onto the nearest table. "How would you like to work for us permanently?"

"What?" Had she heard that right? "You mean a regular job. Something that isn't just for the summer?"

"Exactly. We are expanding the day care and preschool programs to include after-school care. There is so much need for that, and it looks as if it's going to be very popular. Schoolkids need a good place to spend their time while their parents are working, or busy with other family obligations. It wouldn't be a full-time job, at least not to start. But there's a great chance it will work into one eventually. What do you say?"

"I say yes." She couldn't believe it. "Do you really mean this? I'm not dreaming, am I?"

"No chance of that."

"This is an answered prayer. Thank you, Marin. This is so great." Down deep, she realized it was exactly what her heart wanted. She loved being around kids and making sure they had a fun and productive day. She loved her church and her family here. God had been leading her all along, why couldn't she have seen that? Why did she spend all that time worrying about what to do with her life and how things would work out?

What she needed to do was to quit worrying.

"You need to talk with Pastor Michaels to get all the particulars, but I think this is going to be a good fit, don't you?"

"Absolutely."

Her phone jingled. She pulled it out of her jeans pocket. Another text message from Chad. She took the box and began distributing brushes around three of the tables.

Where R U? he'd written.

Where R U? she typed back.

"Who is that?" Marin asked with a note of amusement. "That's not Chad, is it?"

How was she going to answer that? "I'm taking the fifth."

"Ah, so you don't have to hear me go on about where deepening friendships can lead. I got it." Marin winked as she shut the cabinet door. "I'm going to head over for worship. I'll take care of attendance so you can, well, visit with some of the other counselors."

Her phone jangled. "I don't mind helping with attendance."

"Neither do I. You're invaluable here, don't you know that? Go take a few minutes before the service starts and take it easy. We're going to have another wild and woolly day."

"Okay, thanks." She skipped out the door. She wanted to tell herself it was because she had a few free minutes, but really, that wasn't the truth. No, the truth was as complicated as it could get. She squinted in the bright morning sunshine to read Chad's message.

In church. Saved U a seat.

Like I would sit next to U, she typed. The parking lot was packed, and there was a line of cars dropping off kids. A few of the kids called out to her and she waved. Her phone trilled again, with Chad's answer.

Who better?

So he made her laugh. There was nothing

wrong with that. There was just something about him that made her spirit lighter than air. That couldn't be wrong, right? She joined the kids and trooped up the front steps into the shelter of the calm sanctuary. Sunlight blazed through the stained glass windows, gracing the rows of pews with jeweled tones. A shaft of light slanted through the church as if to lead her directly to the spot where Chad was sitting alone, his head bent as he studied his phone and waited for her response.

She pulled over against the wall, well out of the stream of kids and tapped out her answer. Can't think of anyone better than you. She sent it before she could change her mind and delete it entirely.

She watched him chuckle. He looked to be enjoying this exchange—and their friendship—as much as she did.

If that's true, U need to get out more.

She liked his depreciating sense of humor most of all, she realized. She leaned against the wall, watching him sit up straight in the bench and look around. As if he felt her gaze, he turned toward her. His slow smile was about as perfect as a smile could be.

He was about as perfect as a man could be. A real Prince Charming. He was amazingly handsome, inordinately kind, a real gentleman and as wholesome and faithful as a man ought to be. Not to mention he was funny and rich and sensible and real. He was Mr. Dreamy. A hundred on a scale of ten. Was that why he was scaring her so much?

He waved and the distance of the large sanctuary shrunk. The noise and chaos of all those kids getting into their groups and into place faded to silence. Her feet moved toward him. Everything within her stilled until there was complete calm and total peace. His smile made her soul brighten unbearably.

Yes, this was definite trouble. She stumbled in the aisle and his hand caught hers, steadying her, drawing her safely toward him. She gazed into his eyes and saw the kind of man who always stood strong. The kind of man she could always count on.

Not that she wanted a friendship that deep with him. Remembering what Marin, Lucy, Katherine and Ava had told her, she decided right then and there she had to be very careful. Friendship was one thing, but a romance was entirely another. She had to keep the two very separate.

"Thanks," she told him breathlessly as she

slid onto the pew beside him. "I caught my toe."

"It happened to me earlier." His confession was low and rumbling with amusement. "It wasn't fair because I think I distracted you with my dazzling wit."

"Oh, you mean the text messages? Not at all," she quipped, doing her best to keep a straight face. "I was laughing over something else entirely."

Why did that make both of them grin? Maybe because when they were together it was like the perfect day. She muted her phone and stuck it in her pants pocket. How had this happened? She didn't want to have a crush on anyone. She had a policy. She had plans.

"Have you gotten a hold of Lauren about Saturday yet?"

His innocent question felt like a slap. She had meant to tell Lauren. "Not yet."

"Just let me know." Since the pastor had entered, Chad stood.

Rebecca was slow to follow. She had wanted to go out with him more than anything on Saturday night before she realized her true feelings, but what about now? She had to be cautious and careful. She wasn't ready to accidentally fall into another relationship. She was not ready to trust another man with her heart.

All day long, she was troubled. Every time she spotted Chad across the room leading his group in prayer or outside puffing on the referee whistle during soccer or head bent in earnest conversation with a group of kids, her stomach knotted up. She hadn't meant for this crush to happen. She really hadn't. What did she do now? It was a relief at the end of the day to go straight to her car.

Predictably her cell trilled as she was unlocking the door. It was Chad calling this time. She stared at the screen as it rang a second time.

Get real, Rebecca, she told herself. He wasn't asking to marry her. They were just friends. This was nothing serious. Why was she getting so jumpy? That was one question she couldn't answer. Or, truthfully, didn't want to. But she felt better as she answered. "Hi there, buddy."

"Oh, so you are going to talk to me." His footsteps padded behind her on the blacktop. "I wanted to catch you before you left."

She disconnected and turned around. He emerged from the shade of the tree walking with that athletic confidence of his, and he was smiling, but there was something different in his eyes. Something that looked very much like sadness. Had he been watching her debate whether to answer his call or not? Had she hurt him?

"Sorry, I have a lot on my mind," she explained. That was the complete truth. "We didn't have plans for tonight, did we?"

"No, but I was hoping we could start—"

"—cooking lessons." They said the words together.

"It's okay. We can do it another night," Chad was quick to add and pocketed his phone.

Now she felt horrible. "No, tonight is fine. How about we make spaghetti?"

"Sounds great to me. You're sure you don't mind?"

"Mind? No. I'm looking forward to it." And that, she discovered, was true, too.

"You seemed a little distant today. I know you were busy. I was busy, too. It was that kind of day." He shrugged, maybe a little shy and self-conscious.

It only made her like him more. Okay, so she was a little sweet on him. She was just going to have to get used to it and accept it. This wasn't a serious relationship. This wasn't even a relationship. This was a friendship—friends, and nothing more, nothing deeper. Just—what had Chad called it?—summer friends. That's it. They were summer friends.

"It wasn't anything I did, was it?" A tiny crinkle cut into his forehead.

"No. It's me. Entirely me." How did she explain? She didn't even understand it herself. "I'll meet you at my place?"

"Deal." He towered over her for one more moment looking like everything good that a man should be. "I'm going to apologize ahead of time. I don't have a lick of kitchen experience. We had a kitchen staff when I was growing up, and for the last two years I was eating in the dorms. So if I do something like accidentally burn something or catch something on fire, you won't end our friendship, right? Or our cooking lessons?"

"No, I promise." Why was she laughing? And how did this man make her feel as if life was one wonderful, fun adventure? "If you do either of those things, I will see it for the cry for help that it is. I will do my duty and I won't let you go off to cook on your own until we're certain you aren't a danger to yourself or a menace to society."

"Excellent. You're a true friend, Rebecca." He saluted her crisply. "I'll see you in a few."

She watched Mr. Dreamy walk away and thought of how good he was with the day camp kids. They all seemed to really like him. He seemed to fit right in with the other counselors. He was excellent at every sport they had played and he seemed faithful to the core. Of course she had developed a crush for him. What girl wouldn't? Maybe there was nothing wrong with harboring a tiny, harmless crush. After all, it wasn't as if she was going to amend her No Man policy. A crush was just a strong regard. Why shouldn't she spend time with him? Even though he is Mr. Perfect, it's not as if she's going to fall in love with him. She was in charge of her heart, thank you very much. She had no reason to panic.

She was in her twenties, she rationalized as she unlocked her car and started the engine. It was the time for young adults to explore the positive possibilities for their lives and to have a little harmless fun, right? This was the time in her life to make lasting friendships. There was nothing wrong with that.

Maybe the trouble was that she was being way too serious. She lowered the windows and turned the air-conditioning on high. Heat blasted her, and she couldn't help noticing that Chad was already backing his truck out of the parking space. He was leaving without her.

She put the car in Reverse—ouch, the gear-shift was hot. She touched the steering wheel—double ouch. The tips of her fingers felt as if they were burning off, but did that stop her? No. This was lunacy, she thought as she backed up with two fingers on the wheel, and a measure of how much she was looking forward to spending the evening with him.

She was following him out of the parking lot when her cell rang. She hit the speaker button. "Hi, Chad."

"Hey, I forgot to ask. Do we need to stop by the grocery store?"

"I think I can scrape enough spaghetti makings out of my cupboards to make do."

"Okay. Do I need to bring anything else? Iced tea? Paper plates? Dessert?"

"All you need to do is bring yourself." She checked for traffic and pulled onto the side street. "And Ephraim, if he's hanging around your kitchen. We don't want him to starve."

"That sounds fun. I'll drag him along. He has an evening class tonight, but he can stay long enough to pick up a few cooking tips.

He needs it, believe me. This is a good service you are doing."

"You make it sound as if I'm performing some noble task, like joining the armed services or volunteering for the peace corps."

"It's noble to me." His chuckle was pure friendliness. "Hey, I know. I'll bring ice cream. I think we've got a tub of chocolate chip in the freezer."

"That's my favorite flavor."

"Mine, too."

What were the chances? She slowed to a stop behind his gray truck. She could see the back of his head through his back window. There was something striking about him even from this view.

Her phone beeped. It was call waiting. She checked the screen and saw her sister Aubrey's number. She must be back in town! "Chad, I've got another call. I've got to go."

"Sure thing. See you at the condo." He hung up.

Her sister's call rang in. Rebecca followed Chad through the green light and onto the main road that would take her home. "Hi, Aubrey. How was Canada?"

"Stunning. William got some great pictures. He's really excited to develop them and see what he's got. And I came home with something, too."

"Don't tell me, let me guess." Rebecca thought of the wonderful mountain retreat of Aubrey and William's an hour out of town. They had a small herd of horses these days. "A new horse?"

"No, sorry. It's something much better than a horse." Excitement shivered in her soft voice. "We're going to have a baby."

"Aubrey, how exciting." She hit her blinker and turned into the complex. "You and William must be thrilled."

"We're over the moon. I can't seem to do anything but think about this baby. I've got seven whole months to go, and I can't wait."

"Do Mom and Dad know?" She slowed down for a speed bump.

"I called them last night. They were ecstatic. Katherine is excited, too. Our babies will be born four months apart. Won't that be fun?"

She pulled into her driveway and hit the remote. "It sounds perfect to me. Where are you calling from?"

"Gran's house. We stopped to tell her our news and she's making us stay for supper." Aubrey's voice resonated with happiness. "Not that I mind. I'm supposed to be putting my feet up—for some reason she thinks I should rest— but I'm helping shuck the corn. Since I'm going to need both hands, I've got to go."

"I'm glad you called, Aubrey. This is so exciting." She pulled into the garage and killed the engine. "I get to be an auntie again."

"I'll drop you an e-mail tonight. Gran's hosting Tyler's birthday party."

"I know. I've already got his gift all ready to go."

"I'm excited because everyone will be there."

"Everyone?" She hit the remote and climbed out of the car. "Do you mean Mom and Dad are coming back to town?"

"Yep. It will be great to see them. Oh, and quick, tell me about this new boyfriend of yours."

Rebecca rolled her eyes. Really. Why did she know this was coming? She grabbed her duffel. "He's not my boyfriend. Why can't everyone get that one detail right?"

"You know that William and I were friends before we fell in love."

"Yes, I know." Rebecca started to laugh. "I've heard this before. Go shuck some corn and say howdy to William for me."

After they said goodbye, Rebecca disconnected. She had been offered a job and was going to be an aunt again. What a stellar day. She was unlocking the inside door when her cell chimed. It was another text message from Chad.

I'm on your doorstep. Where are you?

Coming, she answered and stumbled into the laundry room. She dropped her bag on the top of the dryer.

Her phone jingled again. She checked the screen as she passed through the kitchen. Whew. Thought U stood me up.

She spotted the two men on her patio. How long had they been standing there knocking? They looked awfully eager. They really must be hungry. She removed the dowel and opened the door.

"I considered standing you up." She stood aside to let them in. "But I didn't want to disappoint Ephraim."

That made them both laugh. It was a good way to start the evening. She accepted the ice cream Chad handed her and led the way to the kitchen.

Chad couldn't remember the last time he'd had so much fun. Rebecca had magically pulled all the ingredients from her freezer, refrigerator and pantry shelf. She had set them both to chopping while she measured the fresh herbs and put the pasta on to cook.

He could have kept everything straight and learned quickly how this all came together except for all the laughter. Ephraim kept telling corny knock-knock jokes, even though Chad pointed out he was never going to get a date if he kept that up. Rebecca told them about her job offer. She had decided to take it, of course.

When it was time to break the ice cream out of the freezer, Ephraim rushed off for his evening class at the college. Chad took the ice-cream scoop from Rebecca and dug into the carton. It was too bad he was alone with her, wasn't it? He decided that being with her was his favorite thing.

"You give good advice, Chad." She set two bowls on the counter next to him. "Working at the church every summer is where my heart has been. And now here is this opportunity to stay year-round."

"I just pointed out a passage to you, that's all." He filled one bowl with big scoops of rich vanilla ice cream and crunchy chocolate chips. "It must be where He has been leading you all along."

"It feels right." She pulled two ice cream spoons from the drawer. "Here I was worrying about what to do with my life, and it's all working out."

"I knew it would." Chad handed her the bowl and got to work filling the second one. "Want to eat this outside? It's too nice to sit inside all evening."

"Plus, if we eat here we have to look at the dirty dishes. I'm not in the mood to clean them right now."

"Especially since I scorched that hamburger, onion and garlic combination to the bottom of that pan." Good thing it was soaking in the sink or it might never come off.

"It happens." Rebecca slipped a spoon into his dish and took the carton when he was done with it. She yanked open the freezer door. "I've been thinking. We should definitely see a movie on Saturday."

"Great." More good news. "I was a little worried you were going to turn me down."

"I wanted to think this through, that's all." She returned the ice cream and flashed him an apologetic smile. "I've never had a friend like you before, that's all. It's different."

"Different good or different bad?"

"Very good, but it's a little scary how we just get along."

He knew what she meant. He wanted to go slow and try to see if this was right, if this was where God was leading him, but mostly if he had a chance with her. Could she understand where he had been and what he'd done? Could she see he had grown into someone different from that lost, reckless and confused kid he'd been?

"I've never jelled with anyone like this," he confessed. His heart quivered at the risk. "We're a lot alike."

"True. Do you know what I think this is?" She stopped to let him open the sliding door for her.

"What?" He waited, feeling a knock of adrenaline. He was no longer thinking *friend* when it came to her. He was thinking *girl-friend*. What were the chances that she was feeling the same?

"I think this is because we're friends." She pulled out one of the fancy iron chairs to her patio set and settled daintily into it. "There's none of this dating nerves and worry. It's nice, isn't it?"

Talk about a letdown. He steeled his chest, tucked away the disappointment and closed the door. Better luck next time, he thought. "Yeah. Real nice."

"You have made me realize something." She looked at ease sitting there, dragging her spoon across the top of her ice cream, gathering a thin sliver of ice cream and chocolate chips.

"I'm afraid to ask what." He took the other chair, feeling a little deflated. He had to remember that she had been recently hurt by love.

"I never realized the guards I put up before." She took a bite of ice cream and savored it. "We were talking about secrets we keep, even without meaning to. I'm guilty of that because I just don't realize. I think I keep everyone at arm's length. If you would have asked me before I would have said oh, no, there's no way. I have friends, family. I'm busy all the time."

"No kidding. You have a lot going on."

"Well, if I take this job I probably won't go back to school, so then I will be less busy. School is more work than work, you know?"

He nodded. He surely did. He dug his spoon into the ice cream, took a bite and let it melt on his tongue while he listened to her. Listening to her was fast becoming one of his favorite things, too.

"When it comes to you, Chad, my guards aren't up like they normally are."

There was at least one piece of good news. "I like hearing that. It's the same for me, too."

"Maybe it's because we agreed to be friends right up front. Whatever the reason, it's wonderful." She dragged her spoon with slow concentration. "It's nice hanging with you."

"I'll second that." He stared hard at the ice cream melting in his bowl and hoped that his regard for her wasn't showing on his face because he was feeling it with the magnitude of an earthquake. He couldn't ignore the tenderness in his heart and it was shaking up his world. He hadn't planned for this, but he had prayed.

He thanked the Lord for that.

Chapter Ten

The last few days had been nothing but wonderful, Rebecca thought as she carried the tub of buttered popcorn into the movie theater. She followed her sister, her husband and Ephraim. She could hear the familiar pad of Chad's gait behind her as they stopped at the foot of the aisle, surveying the available seats.

"Front, back or middle?" Caleb asked.

"How about in the middle?" Chad suggested.

"Sure." Lauren, leading the group, chose an empty aisle and headed for the center. She found a seat and leaned around the others. "Becca, did you know that Gran's invited everyone for Tyler's birthday party tomorrow?"

"Aubrey sent a text message last night with the info."

"Great. You could bring Chad if you want. And Ephraim, you're invited, too."

"Sorry, I've got my parents." Ephraim slid into a seat.

"I've got plans with my uncle and aunt." Chad reached to take the popcorn from Rebecca.

It was a nice gesture so she could settle into a seat next to Ephraim. He handed her a cup of soda first, so she could get it settled before she took back charge of the popcorn. He was a nice guy. He held every door for her. He was considerate. No wonder she had a crush on him. Who wouldn't?

"I'd love to come on Sunday, though," he explained as he took the seat beside her.

Wow. He was close. His elbow gently bumped hers and stayed there, and they were sharing the armrest. Did she move her arm, or just ignore the contact?

"I understand about family obligations." Why did her voice sound strained and a little tinny? She took a sip of soda and tried again. "You would like my grandmother. She's totally fabulous. She's traveled everywhere. She knows just about everyone. She's slowed down quite a bit since we lost Grandpop a few years ago."

"I'm sorry to hear that. I know how hard that is."

She remembered what Lucy had said the night they had stopped by the bookstore. "I adored him. He was a true horse lover. He and Gran taught all of us to ride and we would go on long rides into the mountains. Gran would pack a picnic lunch and we would eat beside a high mountain lake."

"It sounds pretty wonderful." Chad took a handful of popcorn. "What an amazing thing to do. My family never did anything like that. My parents went to dinner parties and the ballet and I stayed home with the nanny until I was old enough to go."

"Surely you had a good connection with them?"

"Oh, I'm not sure you can understand my family. Not with your picture-perfect one." He leaned back in his chair, glad that the lights had dimmed and advertisements began flashing on the screen. "Don't get me wrong. I'm glad you have a great family life, but my mother would have much rather have been having a spa day than being a mom."

"That had to be hard for you. She wasn't the cookie-baking type?"

"No. Although I can see that yours was."

"My mom is fantastic. I love her so much, all I ever have wanted was to grow up to be just like her. I don't think she's ever been to a spa, but she made sure the cookie jar was full, our dinners were tasty and nutritious and she let us all know we were loved very much."

"That sounds idyllic to me. The closest thing I had to a real family was my granddad."

"His loss was doubly hard for you, then."

"Yeah." He would have said more, but the words stuck in his throat. He would have liked to tell her that he wanted the kind of life she had grown up with. That he was sure that if she had been able to meet Granddad, they would have hit it off. There was more he wanted to say, too. He took a long pull of soda and cleared his throat, determined to try. "Granddad had a lot to do with me getting in school and searching for the right path for my life."

"He loved you." It amazed him that she could see that so clearly.

"He did. I didn't make it easy for him most of the time, but I finally started to get it right about the time he got sick. That last year we had together was a good one. I had just started at the university and their home wasn't that far from campus. I spent a lot of time studying in his room, while he read or dozed."

"Something tells me he treasured that time with you." Rebecca took a handful of popcorn and ate it one piece at a time.

He filled his hand with more of the white fluffy stuff. "He left me quite a bit of money in his will. I like to think he trusted the man I had become enough to know I would do the right thing with it."

"Finishing your degree. Volunteering at the church. Planning on attending seminary. Sounds that way to me." Approval warmed her voice and it meant everything.

The previews started and he munched on popcorn, feeling every piece of his life was starting to fit together. Just like a jigsaw puzzle, the pieces were making sense as they took shape and color. He could see where he was going in a way he never had before and it was because of her. She was the reason.

"Hey, you two." Ephraim leaned over to wink. "Arc you through talking yet? I tried to get a word in edgewise, but I don't want to stand in the way of romance."

"Romance?" Rebecca shook her head. "We're just friends."

"Yep, sure you are. I can see that." But

Ephraim shook his head. "Pass me a napkin, would you, Chad?"

"Sure." He had taken a big enough supply for everyone and handed a few over. He and Rebecca might be friends, but he knew they were going to be more. It was just a matter of time. He could wait. He was a patient man.

Another preview started, and he leaned a little closer to Rebecca. He took another handful of popcorn. "What time do you get back from your grandmother's?"

"Probably around six or seven. Why?"

"I thought we could go do something."

"Like what?"

"I noticed a ten-speed bike in your garage. Want to go for a ride?"

"Are you kidding? I'd love to." She settled back in her seat as the movie credits started. The black-and-white picture cast a faint platinum glow.

Just a little help, please, Lord, he prayed. His heart was sure. His soul was sure. Somehow he had found his perfect match. Was there a chance that she could come to feel the same way about him? Hope filled him as he leaned back to enjoy the classic movie at Rebecca's side.

* * *

"I'll walk you to the door." Chad held the passenger door of his pickup open for her and took her hand to help her down.

What a gentleman. It had been a long time since she had been treated this way. Chris had been like this in the beginning, she remembered, attentive and devoted and the perfect gentleman.

Now why was that thought going through her head? She shouldn't be comparing Chad and Chris. Not only was there no comparison, but she still had Chris in her mind somewhere. What she needed to do was to get every thought of him out for good. He was in the past. She never intended to fall for that kind of man again—the seemingly Prince Charming kind.

Although, she thought as her feet touched the cement driveway, Chad would be irresistible *if* she were looking for romance, which she was not.

"Thank you." Did she really sound that breathless? Goodness. "I had a great time, you two."

Ephraim climbed out of the backseat of the truck, closed the door and straightened his pocket protector. "I did, too. We'll have to do this again sometime. I'd better go check my e-mail. See you two later."

"Bye." Rebecca's hand lingered in Chad's a moment too long. It took her a while to realize it. Maybe because whenever she was with Chad, she felt so at ease. Self-conscious, she pulled her hand away. "You don't have to walk me to my door. I can see it from here."

"Sure, but I wanted an excuse to stay with you. I had such a good time, I'm not ready for it to end."

"We have our bike ride tomorrow evening."

"That we do." He jammed his hands in his pants pockets, looking relaxed and at ease. It was nice that he felt this way, too. "I've never enjoyed spending time with anyone the way I do with you."

"Me, too." She stepped onto her porch. It was easier to look in her purse as she fished for her keys instead of at him.

"I've been meaning to ask. Have you heard anything more from your ex?"

"No." She found her keys and sorted through them for her door key. "So far so good. I haven't checked my messages yet, but I think he finally got a clue."

"Good. I think your brother and Caleb helped him to."

"So do I." She turned the key in the dead bolt. "Katherine mentioned that Jack and Danielle's husband, Jonas, paid him a visit, too. I think he understands I really mean it this time. We're over. He'll move on."

"Have you given any thought to a restraining order?"

"I believe he will do the right thing."

"I hope so. You don't need to be troubled like that. Guys like that give the rest of us a bad name." He opened the door for her.

She brushed past him, holding her feelings still. "I'm not painting you with the same brush, Chad."

"No? Then tell me that your no-dating policy doesn't have anything to do with him." He towered in the doorway so sincere and concerned.

She set down her purse on the hall table. How could she deny the deepening friendship between them? "My vacation from romance has everything to do with Chris. You know, you never told me why you have a no-dating policy?"

"I've been trying to avoid the subject." He grinned sheepishly, somehow making him all the more handsome.

"You said that it was complicated." She led

the way into the living room. "Isn't that another word for a relationship that didn't work out?"

"I wouldn't call it a relationship. Every time I started dating someone, they couldn't love me in the end. They didn't understand what I had been through. That's why I took a break from dating. It seemed safer." He sat on the edge of the chair. "At least until I was clear about who I was and what I wanted from life. And especially the kind of woman I wanted to fall in love with."

"It sounds wise. I tumbled into love with Chris when I was too young to know those things. I think he was too young, too. I wanted it to work, until I found out about the secrets in his life." She eased onto the corner of the couch. "I think you're smart to figure out what you want and the kind of person who will be right for you."

"It's more complicated than that. I have to find a woman who can really see me and not the kid I used to be. I didn't have a perfect family like you did."

"Oh, my family isn't perfect, believe me. You probably don't know that we're a blended family. My mom married John when I was three."

"I didn't know." That surprised him. He never would have guessed it.

"Danielle told me that it was harder for her because she was trying to adjust and everyone else was, too. I was too little, and there was no reason for me to adjust. I think I was terribly spoiled, being the baby of the family."

Adored would be more like it. He could see that very plainly. "You and Danielle? I would have figured that you and Lauren were the real sisters."

"That's because you haven't met Danielle. We look a lot alike. Lauren didn't even grow up with us. Her mom took her when she was a toddler. Linda just ran off to Hollywood and stayed there. Lauren only came back to the family a year ago."

"I had no clue." The sisters seemed as if they had been together forever. Some families were able to make things work, he realized, when others fell apart. He had grown up in a family that was more apart than together, but he knew that was a pattern he would not need to repeat. "Your family must be a strong one."

"We're just average, believe me. But we do love one another and that makes the difference. Plus my mom has heart enough to have made our blended family a real one."

"Something tells me you take after your mom."

"I would like to think so, but I'm sure I fall short." She gave a modest shrug of her shoulders.

She had no idea how awesome she was to him. He had put off thinking about dating and marriage. It just seemed like the wise thing to do. His heart ached with tenderness. It was as if his heart had been waiting for this woman to come wholly alive. She was everything he had ever wanted. "I suppose you would like a big family one day. Lots of kids to look after and take care of."

"I always wanted three kids."

"Hey, me, too. That's a pretty good number."

"I think so." She smiled at him. "That is in the far future since I'm not even dating."

"You don't think there's a chance you might amend your policy?"

"I'm a little afraid to." She seemed so at ease. Surely this conversation wasn't making her the least bit nervous.

He was about to disintegrate from anxiety. "Maybe with the right guy you won't be afraid."

"That's the trouble. I don't know if I can

trust myself." She brushed a lock of hair out of her face, looking vulnerable and sweet.

Emotions surged through him with amazing force. He wanted to protect her. He wanted to take care of her. He wanted to make sure she was never afraid or hurt again. Overwhelmed, he sat gasping for air and hoped she didn't notice.

She didn't seem to. "After what you've been through, do you feel that way?"

"S-sometimes." He choked out. "When I'm confused or I'm afraid of making a mistake, I look in my heart and I trust the Lord. He would never steer me wrong."

"I know. I'm afraid that I might mix up what I think with what He's trying to tell me."

"What do you think He's trying to tell you?"

"I don't know exactly, but I'm trying to keep my heart open."

"Good. That's what I'm trying to do, too."

Please, I need your leading, Lord. He squared his shoulders, trying to decide if this was the right time to tell her about his mistakes and what they had cost him. But how? *Help me find the words, Father.*

None came. He was still searching for them when her phone rang. Rebecca rose gracefully from the couch and checked her cordless.

"It's Danielle," she explained. "It's probably about Tyler's birthday tomorrow. Will you excuse me?"

"I'd best get home anyway." Maybe there would be a better time, he reasoned. There was no longer any doubt. He wanted a future with her. He had to tell her about his past. The real question was how? And when?

He would trust in the Lord to find the right way and the right time. His heart and his future and Rebecca's trust in him was at stake.

When I'm confused or I'm afraid of making a mistake, I look in my heart and I trust the Lord. Chad's words stayed with her through the night and into the next day as she joined her family at her grandmother's house in the country. The trouble was that her heart was bruised and no longer exactly whole. She didn't know what it was telling her. It was like driving through fog; she couldn't see a thing.

"What do you think?" Caleb asked from the bench on Gran's back patio. "Red?"

She eyed the balloon bouquet tethered by the ribbons she had been tying. "Definitely red."

"You got it." He chose a red balloon from the package and filled it with helium. "You look a million miles away. Lauren gets that look when she's remembering our wedding plans."

"Oh, I know where you're going with this." Rebecca rolled her eyes, holding back her laughter. "I expected better from you, Caleb."

"I know, but a guy gets curious, too." He tied off the balloon and handed it to her. "I hear things, I've got to admit. There might be one more wedding in the McKaslin clan before year's end."

"Oh, and who exactly would that be?" She couldn't resist. "I didn't even know Spence was dating."

"Ha. That's a good one. Did you hear that, Spence?"

"I heard it." Spence's deep baritone sounded unusually disgruntled. "Why would you say something like that, Becca? You know good and well what I think about marriage."

"That it's one happily-ever-after you're pining away for?" She laughed; she couldn't help it. She was in an exceptionally good mood.

"A fairy tale, that's what it is." Spence frowned over the barbecue where he was squeezing lighter fluid onto the briquettes. "A foolish notion women get into their heads so some poor sap can buy them a house and pay their bills."

"Poor Spence." She tied the ribbon's knot tight on the balloon. "You really don't believe in true love, do you?"

"No. Never. Absolutely not." He struck a match and tossed it into the barbecue. Flames erupted. "Only a fool believes in something like that."

Interpretation: I wish I could.

She knew how Spence felt. She took another balloon from Caleb and tried to ignore the ache of her lost dreams that seemed so foolish now. How had she let herself believe so much in the wrong man? Was it because she wanted to believe in a fairy tale? Or because she didn't? She had fallen for an apparently perfect guy and when he hadn't been, she had been afraid it was her fault. That she wasn't trying hard enough. That she wasn't enough. Then every time he was good to her or kind to her, it was proof that he was as committed as she was. That was one pattern she refused to repeat again.

"That's a little harsh, isn't it, Spence?" Caleb chuckled. "Otherwise, you're calling me a fool."

"Now I never said that directly." Spence scowled less. He wasn't a man given to mirth.

"You know I'm happy for you and Lauren. She's a good kid. She needs someone like you."

"And I need her." Caleb tied off another balloon. "Rebecca, think this is the last one? I must have blown up a hundred or so."

There were so many balloons, they blotted out the swatch of sky between the patio railing and canopy of trees. "I think we can call it good. I'll distribute them around."

"Great." Caleb stood up from the bench and stretched. He'd been sitting there a long time.

As she unwrapped a handful of balloons from the railing, she thought about the friends thing, how her sisters, Marin and Lucy had said true love was based on friendship. She remembered long ago Lauren saying the same thing about when she first fell for Caleb. They had just meshed, she'd said at the time. He's the best friend she'd ever had.

It was sort of too late to rethink her friends clause with Chad. She knotted the dozen ribbons in her hand around the back of the birthday boy's chair. Across the patio table she saw Aubrey and William on the far side of the yard gathering roses from Gran's incredible flower garden.

Dark-haired William was holding the shears and leaning close to clip the flower

Aubrey braced for him. They looked so sweet and happy together. He clipped the bud and laid it in the small basket she carried over her arm. She blushed prettily. The look they shared was a deeply loving one. She knew if she were to ask Aubrey, her sister would say the same thing. We're best friends first.

Rebecca sighed. Maybe her friends idea wasn't so smart. Her phone jingled. A text message from Chad? Her heart leaped and a quiet, deep joy rushed into her soul. She knew there was only one explanation for that, but she decided to stay in denial for a while.

How goes the party?

We're waiting for the birthday boy. Missed U at church. She typed and sent and, when she heard footsteps coming around the corner, slipped her phone into her pocket.

"What has put such a smile on your face?" Mom wanted to know as she held out her arms wide. "Oh, baby, it's good to see you."

She stepped into her mother's hug and held on tight. "It's good to see you, Mom. You're looking tan."

"We've been having a high time." Mom stepped back and took Rebecca's hands, appraising her with motherly care. "You look beautiful and happy, and here I worried that all that nonsense with Chris would bring you down, sweetie."

"I'm fine. It's over. I'm glad you two didn't come home on my account. Hi, Dad." Her heart warmed as it always did for her dad. John McKaslin gave her a shy kiss on the cheek. He'd always been shy when it came to showing affection, but his heart was big. "How far did you two get this time?"

"We spent way too much time nosing around antique stores in Wyoming." Dad's gruffness was feigned. His eyes were twinkling. "You know Dorrie and antiques."

"I got some great new Depression glass pieces for your set and the one I started for Lauren." Mom looked so pleased. "Oh, there's Spence. I've got to go torture him with a great big hug."

"I've got to get these balloons put up before Tyler gets here."

"I'll torture him and be back to help." Mom traipsed off. "C'mon, John. You need to talk to Spence. He looks peaked. He's working too hard."

"I'll talk to him," Dad promised as he trailed Mom.

Rebecca watched the people she loved. Spence was feigning indifference, as if he didn't need a hug from his parents. Mom began fussing over him, smoothing his hair which she said was too long, pinching his cheeks and commenting on his health. Gran pattered out of the back door with a small covered tray.

"This looks so festive, Rebecca." In a lemon yellow pantsuit, lovely as always, Gran gave an approving smile. "Tyler will be so pleased. Dani called to say they were on their way. Ava isn't here with the birthday cake yet."

"I'll call her and see what's keeping her."

"That would be a help, dear." Gran set the tray on the table and began fussing with the place settings.

Rebecca tied the balloons on the fencing that bordered one edge of the patio and pulled her phone out of her pocket. Just as she was about to dial, a text message came in. Of course she had to read it. She didn't want to admit that she missed Chad. Missing him. There was no rationale for that.

Can't wait for our ride.

Uh-oh. She tried not to listen to the voice of doom whispering in her ear. She wanted to stay in denial about what was happening to her heart for a little while longer.

Me, too, she typed. It was much less than

she felt. Much less than she wanted to say. And all at once so much more. She felt as if she were taking the first step off the edge of the Grand Canyon. Foolishly marching ahead when any smart person would take a huge jump back and stay safe on solid ground.

"They're here!" came a cry from inside the house. The back door slapped open and Ava emerged carrying her cake board and the colorful dog-shaped cake she had baked just for the occasion. Her husband trailed after her, holding her bag, her purse and her cake-decorating case.

Rebecca grabbed another handful of balloons. As Tyler raced around the corner and into sight, hopping with excitement, she joined in the rousing rendition of the happy birthday song. But where were her thoughts?

On Chad and awaiting his next text message. What was she going to do about that?

Chapter Eleven

When she pulled into her driveway, Chad was waiting for her with his top-of-the-line mountain bike glinting in the evening sunshine. She hit the remote and seeing the welcoming smile on his face filled her with an entirely new emotion. She had never felt it before. It swept through her heart and brimmed over into her soul. It was like holding peace in the palm of her hand.

She lowered the window. "Hey, buddy. You look ready and revved to go."

"You said you were on your way. I didn't want to waste a minute of this evening. Tomorrow is back to work, you know. I'll be worn out from the kids and I won't have energy for a long ride."

"Tell me about it." She'd had the best fun

exchanging text messages with him through-out Tyler's party. Seeing him brought home exactly how much she liked him—no, cared about him. She had to be honest with herself. She cared about him very much. "How did your aunt's cake turn out?"

"After my cousins ran by the oven playing baseball you mean? It was flat as a pancake but it tasted great." Chad grinned at her. "It's my belief that chocolate frosting will make anything better."

"I like the way you think." She smiled and he did, too. It was like a little connection between them, something more than a smile. They were one the same wavelength. Seeing him was like the best thing that had happened in a very good day. "I'll just—"

"—pull in and get changed."

He finished her thought perfectly. "I will get your bike down from the hooks and check your tire pressure while I wait. How about that?"

"That would be great." She drove into the shade of the garage, her thoughts jumbling. This man seemed way too good to be true.

She thought of her sisters today and how happy everyone was. Aubrey and William, inseparable, alight with joy expecting their first child. Ava and Brice, how they seemed to be able to finish each other's sentences. Katherine and Jack and their gentle loving regard for one another. Danielle and Jonas, how connected they were with those tender looks and kind words and their abiding love. Lauren and Caleb, so alike down to the soul. Even Mom and Dad with their strong love, always knowing what the other one needed before it was spoken.

They made it seem as if everything that was too good to be true was real, after all.

A little hope crept into her soul. She climbed out of the car and fetched the plastic containers from the backseat.

"Cookies and birthday cake," she explained. "I felt bad that you were left out. Especially considering the demise of your aunt's much-awaited sponge cake."

"I appreciate that." He chuckled. The width of the car separated them, but they seemed closer than ever. "That will give us something to snack on later."

Us. She didn't miss that. She closed the door. "I'll just take these in with me, then. I'll see you in a few."

"It's hot out there. Don't forget to bring a water bottle."

"I won't." She knew she was smiling wider

than was humanly possible because of the way her face felt stretched. Her soul did, too.

Joy followed her into the house where she changed into a pair of denim shorts and a T-shirt. She slathered on sunblock and grabbed a baseball cap, working quickly so she could get back to him.

As she rinsed and filled her water bottle, she could hear faint sounds coming from the garage. It sounded as if he were filling her tires with the hand pump that had been on the shelf next to the bike hooks. She had never realized what a comfort it was to have a guy around who would volunteer to do things for her.

That made it harder than ever not to care about him more, especially when she opened the garage door to lock up and there he was, checking the tire pressure, kneeling on the cement floor looking like her deepest, most secret dream. He had a broad-shouldered competence, as if he could handle any burden. He looked up from his work with an easy grin—he was always in a good mood. He always had a smile to offer her.

Her heart swelled. She was in huge trouble. It looked as though her friend-only clause had backfired.

"You look ready to hit the road." He

straightened up, pump in hand, and returned it neatly to its shelf. "I didn't know if you had a route in mind. I've ridden north of the city, since that's where my aunt and uncle live, but that's a little far from here."

"I happen to have a few suggestions." She locked the door behind her and slipped her door key into her pocket. She grabbed her helmet from the hook and put it on. "I used to belong to a bike club back when I had much more time than I do now."

"Then you know all the best rides." He pushed her bike out onto the driveway. "Okay, you pick."

"How about we head toward the university and out past the museum?" She hit the garage door button and took off at a sprint. She hopped over the sensors and took her bike from him. "There's a back road that goes on forever into the prettiest country around. And it's not too hilly."

"Sounds perfect."

When he smiled, she realized that her heart did, too. Perfect. Yes, that was the word. She put her foot on the pedal, gave her bike a push and hopped on. She led the way through the complex and down the residential streets, knowing Chad was a few paces behind her, a welcome companion on this illuminating day.

"I need a time-out." Chad called out at the base of the hill.

Up ahead of him, Rebecca's foot came down and she glanced over her shoulder at him. "You just don't want to climb another slope."

"I timed my request perfectly, if I do say so myself." And he wasn't ashamed of it. He swung to the ground and nudged the bike far onto the gravel shoulder. There hadn't been much traffic on this forgotten country road, but it was better to be safe than sorry. "I thought you said this way wasn't hilly."

"I said not *too* hilly." She hung her helmet on her handlebars. "There's a difference."

"Great." He laughed. Laughter came easily whenever he was around her. He took off his helmet and unhooked the bottle from his bike frame. He took a long pull of water. "It's been a while since I've put in this much cycling."

"You mean you spend time at the gym, and that's fine, but there's nothing like getting out on the road for a tough workout." Rebecca had her water bottle in hand and she hopped across the shallow ditch to the grassy meadow beyond. "I'm glad you wanted to stop. My muscles are jelly. I have to admit I didn't want you to think I was a wimp, so I've been pushing a little harder than I'm used to."

"It's catching up to you, huh?"

"Is it." She dropped into the soft grass, framed by wildflowers.

He'd never seen anything lovelier. Tender feelings rose up within him and floated like clouds in the sky. He sat down beside her in the soft grass. "It's catching up to me, too. I'm impressed with you."

"With me?"

"You're a powerhouse. My quads were jelly about two miles ago."

"Sure." She didn't look as if she believed him, but she blushed. "It's nice of you to say. You don't seem to mind if a girl can keep up with you."

"I don't. I like that we're compatible."

"Me, too." She smiled. "I haven't been biking in a long time. It's been tough finding someone who thinks a twenty-mile ride on a ninety-degree day is fun."

"I take it you didn't do this often?"

"I usually go by myself."

Ah, not with the ex. Chad didn't know why

that mattered to him, but it did. "So, now that I know this about you, I have to ask. What else do we have in common?"

"I don't know." She popped the top of her water bottle and took a dainty sip. With the pink baseball cap shading her heart-shaped face and the blush of heat and happiness on her cheeks, she looked adorable. Simply adorable.

The tenderness in his chest intensified a notch.

"You know I love swimming and volley-ball." She took another sip of water and set her bottle aside. "I'm fairly decent when it comes to baseball and basketball."

"That doesn't surprise me." He braced his arms and leaned back a little, delighting in watching her. "I'm fond of baseball and bas-ketball, too. What's a little-known fact about Rebecca McKaslin?"

"One of my favorite hobbies is cross-stitching."

"Sadly, I can't say the same." He loved it when they laughed together. "I like to hang on my computer."

"I should have known you were a computer geek. You hang out with Ephraim."

"True. I'm minoring in computer science. Do you have a computer?"

"Yes, but I mostly use it for school, which means it's on summer break, too. I suppose you're one of those people who are brilliant enough to actually tell your computer what to do, instead of praying that it works at all, like me."

"I don't know about that. I've done my share of praying. How did the birthday bash turn out? Your text messages left out a lot of details."

"Tyler was in seventh heaven. He got a ton of presents and best of all, my parents are back in town. He's fond of his grandparents. Then Ava made a Dalmatian-shaped cake. It looked just like Lucky. Tyler was thrilled."

"That's what a kid needs. A pet to grow up with."

"I think so, too. He's a fairly new addition to the family, and Danielle is taking the adjustment in stride. Lucky actually has as much energy as Tyler does, so they are a good match. They are best friends already."

"Best friends. That sounds about right." Maybe he wasn't thinking so much of Rebecca's nephew as he was of their relationship. That's where they were heading. That's where he wanted things to go. He wanted to be best everything with her. Never had his future been so clear—or his heart.

"What are your aunt and uncle like?"

"They are the nicest people. When I was troubled, they were always the ones I could talk to. Every summer, their place was more home than my house was. When my dad took off, they became my refuge. The only place that was sane."

"When did your dad take off?"

"Two days before my fifteenth birthday."

"Ouch," she sympathized. The breeze danced through her hair. She was graced by sunshine and she looked sweetly precious.

I'm in love with her. The realization struck him like a sudden blow. He took a shaky breath and let the truth settle in. Love. It came like a gift to his heart. It was a strength of emotion he had never felt before.

"I'm sorry that happened to you." She laid her hand on his.

Comfort filled him. "I got through it eventually. It was pretty tough for a while. For a time there I lost my way."

"I'm glad your aunt and uncle were there for you. I'm glad you found your way." Her eyes turned luminous. It was so easy to read her caring for him. "If you hadn't, I doubt we ever would have met. And that would be a shame."

His love for her stretched as wide as the sky and as strong as the Rocky Mountains, immovable in the distance.

Please Lord, he prayed, let her feel this way, too. He had never wanted anything as much as her love.

"It surely would be," he agreed, gathering up his courage. Maybe this would be the right time to tell her.

"I'm ready to go. How about you?" She grabbed her water bottle and took one last sip.

"Sure." He had barely got the word out before she bounced up like a sunbeam and brushed bits of grass off her clothes.

The moment had passed. He grabbed his water and tried to think of how to bring up the subject. But she was already hopping across the ditch and crunching in the gravel toward her bike. She reached for her helmet.

Maybe there would be a better opportunity, he thought.

"Should we turn around?" She buckled on her helmet. "Or do you want to go another mile?"

"You decide." He said those fateful words knowing full well she would ask him to pedal another mile uphill, but he didn't mind. As long as he was with her, that was what mattered.

Beneath the outdoor umbrella of a coffeehouse near the university, Rebecca glanced over her shoulder to watch Chad. He was at the register paying for their drinks. How could it be possible that she was with someone like him? He had her father's manners and her brother's competence and yet there was something both familiar and different about him. Being with him just felt right, effortless. She could just be herself. It was a wonderful feeling. And terrifying.

Don't think about what this means, she told herself. Maybe she should just enjoy this time with him.

"A strawberry Italian soda with whipped cream as ordered." Chad set the tall plastic cup down on the little table. He was carrying a similar cup, different color soda.

"Blueberry?" she guessed.

"I have a weakness for blueberries."

She would have to remember that. "My sister has this to-die-for recipe for blueberry scones. I could make some for you."

"I wouldn't say no." He settled into the

chair across from her. "You could throw in one of your cooking lessons. I could try to fry eggs and bacon. What do you think?"

"For dinner?"

"Sure. You name the night, and I'll bring the groceries."

"I'll check my calendar and get back to you. My parents are in town and I don't know what they've got planned." She took a sip of the sweet creamy treat. "I'm going to have to bike another five miles to burn this off."

"Save it for the court tomorrow." He winked. "Basketball. I know we're not playing against each other, but I'm betting the girls will keep you running."

"I'll be reffing. I'm sure I'll be worn to a frazzle." She grinned. Yes, she definitely loved her job. She had listened to her heart, doing what she loved, and the good Lord had provided. Would this—with Chad—work out, too? "I'm sorry I got a muscle cramp. I stretched my calves well."

"No need to apologize. I was on the verge of collapsing, so you did me a favor by wanting to stop and cool down." He took a long swallow. "Is that your phone?"

"I think it's been doing that all along." She pulled her cell out of her pocket. "It's

Ava. She's probably calling to torment me further. I'm going to call her back later. You were a huge topic of conversation at the birthday bash."

"You didn't mention anything about that when we were texting."

"Limited space." She quipped. She took a sip of the drink and let the strawberry richness spill across her tongue. "I would have suggested stopping at Ava's bakery, but that would only further the speculation."

"Speculation?"

She blushed. How on earth could she tell him about everyone's theory about friends and romance? What would he think if he knew? She wasn't ready to admit the truth to herself much less to him.

"My sisters are all happily married and think that I ought to join their ranks."

"Funny. My aunt and uncle were curious why my phone kept beeping. For some reason they thought I had a girlfriend." He grinned so that all his dimples showed. "They didn't believe our friend policy for a second."

"Neither did my parents. I—" A weird sensation trickled down her neck. She turned around to see Chris on the other side of the glass door to the patio, his hand on the handle, his gaze fastened on her.

She knew that look. His eyes were dark and cold. His mouth was pulled down into an angry frown. He looked as tense as if he'd been carved out of marble. Whatever she'd been about to say fled from her mind. All she could remember was the last time she had seen that expression on Chris's face.

Fine fear trembled through her. This was different from the day he had come up to her at the mailboxes. Hate radiated off him like cold from a glacier. He had been that way the day he had wrapped his hands around her arms and lifted her off her feet. His enraged words, demanding money, telling her how he was tired of her goody-goody act, echoed in her brain.

She was dimly aware of a chair scraping against the concrete. A shadow fell across her. Chad, she realized, towered over her like a knight in shining armor. Protective, he planted himself between her and Chris. His message was clear. Chris dropped his gaze, turned around and disappeared back inside the coffee shop.

Her heart soared. "Thanks, Chad."

"No problem." He circled around to his

chair, but kept his gaze on the door. "That was a surprise. At least he stayed away from you."

"That's all I want."

"Are you all right?" He reached across the table and took her hands in his. It was a tender gesture and as comforting as anything she'd ever known.

Her hands weren't shaking for the reason he thought. The way he treated her, and the way hc looked out for her, how he behaved toward her spoke more loudly than any words.

I'm falling for him, she realized. Big-time.

Her phone rang again. She snatched it out of her pocket to peek at the screen. "This is my mom. Do you mind?"

"Not at all." He leaned back in his chair and sipped at his drink.

He was dcfinitely a nice change. She leancd back in her chair, too, and answered. "Hi, Mom."

"Hi, baby. I hope I'm not interrupting anything."

Why did Mom sound so hopeful that she was? Funny. Rebecca reached for her soda. "You're not interrupting one bit. What are you up to?"

"I'm on our patio with John. He made us some sun tea and we're sitting here watching the evening go by. I wanted to see if you wanted to ask that new boyfriend of yours—"

"Friend, Mom." Rebecca rolled her eyes. Across the table, Chad met her gaze and his dimples flashed with amusement.

"You know that's how it was at first with John and me." Mom didn't even try to disguise how pleased she was. "When we met, it was *like* at first sight. We just clicked. It felt so right. We were instant friends and that friendship developed into a deeper and deeper bond that has been one of the best blessings in my life."

"Mother." Rebecca could not believe her mom was doing this, too. "Please don't tell me *this* is the reason you're calling me."

Mom laughed. "No. I just thought a word of advice wouldn't be out of line. I called to invite that friend of yours to dinner at our town house next Sunday."

"I thought you would be heading back out on the road." Rebecca bit her bottom lip to keep from laughing. She didn't know what was so funny or why, but Chad was doing the same thing.

"Oh, we're staying in town for the rest of the summer. Katherine might need us with Jack putting in so many hours to cover vacations." Mom paused for a second. "I have this terrible feeling that I am interrupting. You are with him right now, aren't you?"

How was she going to answer that?

"Oh, I'd better go and leave you two be. Don't forget to ask him to supper. I'll talk at you later, baby. Bye, now." Mom sure sounded pleased.

"Bye." Rebecca disconnected and pocketed her phone. "I wonder how long it will take until the rest of the family is calling me."

"Think we'll have a chance to make it home?" He sure seemed to be enjoying this. Of course, an only child who did not understand the pressures of having five older siblings would think the situation was amusing.

"Are you kidding?" She climbed to her feet. "We'll be lucky to make it out to the bikes."

As if to prove her point, her phone began ringing the instant they reached the sidewalk. She checked the screen. "See? What did I tell you? It's Gran calling."

Chad appeared entertained. "You have a fun family. You're pretty immersed, aren't you?"

"Probably just a tad. Nothing serious, just enough to justify their nosiness." Bless them. She loved her family. They were everything in the world to her. "I really should take this."

"Sure. Hand me your key and I'll unlock us both."

He held out his hand, palm up, and she tugged the key out of her pocket. Their fingers brushed, and rare sweetness wrapped around her.

"Take your time," he told her as he bent to release the bikes from the stand. "It's your grandmother. She deserves all your attention."

"I knew there was a reason I liked you, Chad Lawson." Yes, she was definitely out of excuses and every last piece of denial.

There was no way to ignore the crest of affection that nearly toppled her over. She leaned against the wall of the coffeehouse, found her balance and answered her phone.

Chapter Twelve

"Hey, stranger."

Rebecca looked up from her piece of pizza to the handsome man striding toward her through the shadowed church grounds. Her spirit brightened simply at seeing him. No surprise there. She was finally starting to accept it. "I was hoping you would come sit with me. Your boys have kept you busy so far today."

"Busy, sure, but I'm having a blast." Chad set his plate and juice box on the table and sat. He looked relaxed and happy, as if he was right where he belonged.

"Working with kids seems to suit you." She took a bite of pizza and reached for her napkin.

"It's a good fit." He stopped to bow his head for a silent grace, and reached for his soda. "I knew I would be happy here."

"This is like your dream job."

"Exactly. And my stamina is improving, just like you said it would. I've got some energy left. I'm starting to adjust."

"I never had a single doubt," she said and they shared a smile.

"Now I need to finish my bachelor's degree and seminary." He took another long drink. "I can't wait for September to roll around so I can get started."

"You like school?"

"I like learning."

"Me, too." She reached for her cup.

Don't look at the future. She willed down the images struggling to life in her mind. She would not get ahead of herself. She wouldn't wonder what it would be like to be married to a minister.

No, she was going to stay sensible and in control of her heart.

She took a cooling sip of cherry lemonade. "That's probably why I've stayed in school for so long. I love everything about college. The classes, the research papers and even the exams. I don't like the exams themselves, but I love preparing for them."

"I like that every day is never exactly the same. There's always something new to learn and something different to do. That's what I like about this job, well, aside from working with the kids."

"It is fun. Challenging, but fun." She hadn't realized it, but they were kindred spirits. Alike in so many ways, and even where they were different, it was a compliment. "I'm psyched about getting to do this all year long."

"I'm psyched for you."

She believed him. He wasn't just being kind, he was truly glad for her. It showed in the warmth of his voice, in the honesty in his eyes and the way he seemed to focus on her. As if no matter what, he would always be on her side rooting for her.

Which was pretty nice, since that was how she felt about him, too.

"So Rebecca, what's on your agenda for tonight?"

"I'm going to go over to Gran's." Was it her imagination or did he look disappointed? Rebecca shared his reaction. She loved her grandmother and wasn't going to let her down, but the thought of being apart from Chad was a depressing one. She mentally rolled her eyes. Yikes. Was she in love or what?

Yes. She contemplated the pepperoni

rounds on her piece of pizza. "Why? What did you have in mind?"

"Nothing specific. I thought we could hang out together."

"That sounds nice." She gathered up her courage. "I told Gran I would come help her with her garden. Spence and Lauren usually help her with the grounds and she has a gardener come in weekly, but she likes to putter and asked me to keep her company."

"You're blessed to have a grandmother who loves you."

"Don't I know it." She thought about how lonely his growing-up years must have been and all that he was missing now. But that wasn't the reason behind her sudden idea. "Why don't you come? I'm sure Gran would love to meet you and we could always use another set of hands. There's a lot of weeding and picking to be done."

"Are you sure I wouldn't be in the way?"

"How could you even think that?"

"I just wanted to make sure. Your grandmother might not want some guy hanging around when she's planning on quality time spent alone with one of her favorite granddaughters."

"We're all her favorite grandchild, believe

me. She's that kind of grandma." And just to put him at ease, she fished her cell out of her pocket. "Why don't I give her a call and warn her that you're coming."

"That's fair. If she says it's all right, then I'll come. I've never pulled weeds before, but I'll do my best."

And his best, she reasoned, was probably a far sight more than most. She scrolled through the numbers and hit Gran's. "You have never gardened?"

"I've never actually been in a garden. Flower gardens, you know. Those museum kind of gardens with greenhouses? I've been in those. But not a vegetable garden. At least, I'm assuming that's what you're talking about."

"Yes. You're in for a treat. Pulling weeds is like the most fun experience a person can have."

"Now you're pulling my leg. You're mocking the garden-challenged."

"Not at all. I'm trying to build up your anticipation for the evening. So you're looking forward to it."

"Instead of regretting that I have agreed to trade my leisurely evening for hard physical labor?"

"Exactly." Gran wasn't answering, so she left a message and pocketed her phone. "Why are you trading your comfortable evening for working in my grandmother's garden?"

"Good question. I *could* say I'm a workaholic, but that wouldn't be the truth." It was hard to tell what he was hiding as he stared down at his plate.

She had no right to hope. They had agreed to be friends only. He had said he wasn't dating right now. She dug in to her second piece of pizza. Hadn't he also said he was thinking about starting to date again? Her pulse fluttered with part fear and part hope as he lifted his gaze.

His heart was in his eyes. Full and tender and revealing. "The truth is, I would like to meet this grandmother of yours. I would like to spend the evening with you."

Her fear drained away leaving hope to flourish.

"That sounds perfect." Suddenly shy, she took a bite of pizza before she said more than she was ready to admit.

Chad nodded slowly, as if he understood exactly what she kept to herself. His tender look told her that she was not alone in her feelings.

* * *

All afternoon long a growing worry began to gnaw at her. Every time she caught sight of Chad, whether he was reffing the boys' basketball games or sitting in a circle on the shady grass leading a prayer group, the love she felt for him shimmered like a new star.

During her afternoon break, she grabbed a banana from her bag and gave Lauren a call. While she waited for the phone to connect, she wandered through the grounds toward one of the flower gardens, where several benches offered an inspirational retreat. She hunkered down in a private spot and was ready to disconnect when she heard Lauren pick up.

"Whew. Hi, Becca. Are you still there?"

"Yes. Is this a bad time?"

"Other than the fact that Spence is glaring at me across the bookshelves, no." There was a thump in the background. Lauren must be shelving new books. "What's up? Aren't you at work?"

"I actually took one of my breaks."

"Shocking."

"I know." She leaned against the wrought iron arm and put her feet up on the bench. "I needed to ask you something."

"Sure, just wait a sec, okay? I'm going to

be impervious to Spence's frown. It drives him nuts." There was another thump. "Now he's storming away. We can talk in privacy."

"Good. The last thing I want is for Spence to overhear any of this."

"Oh no, not Chris again."

"No, although I did see him. Wait, that's a story for another time." She had limited time. She had to stick to the point. "I need your honest opinion, no holds barred, even if it hurts my feelings."

"You've got it. What's going on?"

"I'm in love with Chad." She heard the shocked silence on the other end and squeezed her eyes shut. "I shouldn't have blurted it out like that. It sounds so serious, and I haven't even let myself think too much about it."

"Love is serious. If you're looking for a reaction, I think that's great. Chad seems like a good guy."

"He really does." She opened her eyes, and it wasn't the serene rosebushes and lilies nodding in the breeze that she saw. It was Chad the afternoon she'd first seen him carrying a box of books. Her first impression then had been a good one. Her opinion of him had only gone up from there. "It's as if we're perfect together."

"That's how I see it." There was a final thunk and a rustle, as if Lauren had given up shelving entirely and had sat down to devote her full concentration to the call. "Chad seems like a really nice guy. When we all went out to the movie, I noticed how he treated you. He held every door for you. He paid for your movie and popcorn and drinks."

"He was so nice then. He gets nicer to me every time we are together."

"And the way he looked at you. Wow."

"Really?" She hadn't been aware of it. Maybe because she had been busy reminding herself how they were only friends and things had to stay that way. When she looked back, maybe down deep she had known all along how right they were together. Why else would she have been so worried about staying friends? "How did he look at me?"

"As if you are his dream come true."

Double yikes. That only fueled her panic. Rebecca took a deep breath to steady herself.

"I think you two are right for each other. You both like the same things. You both have similar senses of humor. You have similar beliefs and values in life. He's like the perfect guy."

"I know." Wasn't that the trouble? "The last time I thought someone was so perfect for me, it was Chris. What if I'm wrong? What if I have lousy judgment and I'm doomed to having disappointing relationships?"

"You've been hanging around Ava too long," Lauren sympathized. "There is no doom. You don't have lousy judgment. Chris made the choices he did in how he treated you and how he lived his life. You had nothing to do with that."

"Chad seems perfect, too. I want to believe, don't get me wrong." She traced her finger along the edge of the bench railing. "I don't want to get hurt."

"There are no guarantees, but you have to ask yourself what is different this time with Chad. Is this love something your heart and soul is telling you, or something you are trying to make fit?"

Hours later while seated in Chad's truck as he pulled into her grandmother's driveway, she was still mulling over Lauren's question. Okay, so she already knew the answer.

There was no denying the truth. Her love for him just was—it was precious and tender and brand-new. She didn't have to try to change herself for it to fit. She didn't have to try to change who she was for Chad's affection.

Perhaps this was good enough to be true.

True love had happened to everyone else in her family—except for poor Spence. Maybe it was finally her turn. Maybe God had answered her prayer and she should accept this great blessing to her life, open her heart and take one day at a time with Chad. See where this was leading her.

"You're sure quiet." Chad glanced over at her as he navigated the private country driveway. "You're not regretting bringing me along, are you?"

"Never. What a thought. Nothing could be further from my mind."

"Oh, does that mean you've been thinking how glad you are that I'm here?" He shot her a charming grin.

Her heart somersaulted. Yep, she was pretty susceptible to his charm, probably because she loved him. The tender look he gave her was the exact match for the tenderness she felt for him.

She rolled down the window and let the hot August breeze blow against her face. It tangled in her hair and scorched her skin, but the fresh grass-scented air reminded her of all the joys in her life she had let slip by her. Too busy with school and then too busy with her job. Worried over Chris and then the breakup.

How come she seemed to notice how full of joy the world was and wanted to take the time to appreciate it whenever she was with Chad?

That was just another sign. "I'm taking the fifth."

"You plead the fifth amendment a lot, Rebecca."

"Because it's safer being silent than admitting to some feelings."

"Like caring feelings?" he asked, waiting.

"Exactly." She spoke the word before she'd realized it. She blushed and looked out the window. Vulnerability washed over her like the breeze. She had opened her heart just like that.

"I could say the same thing." His answer vibrated deep and quietly as he pulled the truck to a stop in the gravel turnaround in front of the house. "I'm going to plead the fifth, too."

He reached across the console and covered her hand with his much bigger one. His touch felt solid and dependable, as if there wasn't anything she couldn't trust him to do. When she gazed up at him, she saw a man she could grow old with, laughing all the way.

"Your grandmother's coming." Chad nodded toward the wraparound porch where a slim figure moved through the shade beneath the roof's outcropping. "How are you going to introduce me?"

She felt what he was asking, which was much more than his words could say. Fear skidded down her spine and she pushed it away. She was not afraid. She was sure beyond all doubt. "I have a few options. I could say that you're a stray I found alongside the road."

He chuckled. "Or?"

"Or I could say you're the new chauffeur I hired to drive me around."

"That's the one I would go with." He winked at her and leaned across her to open her door. "It would be great if you would wait for me to come help you down."

"I can do that on my own."

"I know," he shot over his shoulder as he closed the door. He kept an eye on her through the windshield as he circled the truck.

"Hello there, young man!" Gran called out from the top step. "It's so good to finally meet you."

"I'm glad to be here, ma'am."

Rebecca watched, jaw dropping, as Chad held out his hand and helped her frail grandmother down the steps like a gentleman of old.

"What a nice young man you have here,

Rebecca." Gran beamed as she walked with her hand on Chad's arm, carefully stepping in the loose gravel. "I approve of this one."

"Good to know, Gran. Thanks." She bit her lip, watching the blush steal across Chad's face—and the joy, too. There was an unmistakable joy. "This is one boyfriend I just might keep."

"Boyfriend?" Chad held out his hand, palm up, to help her down from his truck. "I like the sound of that."

"So do I." The hope rising within her seemed to take wing. Her feet hit solid ground but her heart and her soul felt light as the fluffy white clouds sailing high overhead.

She accepted Chad's other arm and the three of them retreated to the shade of the porch. The hot breeze blew the sweet scent of blooming roses from the flower beds and ripening fruit from the nearby orchard. It felt wonderful to be at his side.

"I hope you kids haven't eaten yet," Gran was saying as she led the way around the corner to the kitchen door. "I have chicken marinating for the barbecue. Chad, you look like a capable young man. How good of a barbecuer are you?"

"I can get the job done." He held the door

for Rebecca, too. Their gazes met. They both bit their lips to keep from laughing.

"Perfect."

"Gran? Now that you've got Chad on barbecue duty, what do you need me to do?"

"I need you in a supervisory capacity, dear. Someone has to keep an eye on this young man."

"I do need supervision," he agreed, laughing. He couldn't help it. He hadn't been this happy in a long time.

"You're right, Gran." Rebecca gave him a merry look as she passed by. "I'll keep him in line. Do you want us to go fetch some fresh veggies before we put him to work?"

"That would be a help." The fragile, stylish older lady pushed a lock of silver hair behind her ear and headed for the refrigerator. "Chad, I hope you like chocolate pie. I picked up one at Ava's shop this morning. My, but her place has gotten busy."

"How is Ava? I haven't returned her call from last night," Rebecca said as she handed him a cloth basket, which he gladly took. Since she was heading toward the kitchen door, he opened that for her and earned her smile.

"She wasn't at the bakery when I was

there. It's not like her to miss a day of work. I called and left a message on her voice mail."

"You know how she is. She forgets to return messages." Rebecca slipped past him with a smile and a crook of her finger. "Gran, Chad and I won't be long."

He closed the screen door behind them and followed Rebecca down the side steps. It was like stepping into paradise. Vines of roses climbed a pristine white fence and archways. Mature trees swayed solemnly in the breeze. He took in the enormous garden in neat rows, lush and plentiful. Horses, grazing in the far field, lifted their heads from the grass in curiosity. One horse gave a neigh and stomped its foot.

"Hi, Tasha!" Rebecca called out. "I promise I'll save the corn husks for you."

The horse nodded her head in a regal manner, as if that was the least Rebecca could do, and went back to her grazing.

He followed her into the rows of tall stalks where tasseled ears of corn were plump and fragrant. "You spent your summers here, didn't you?"

"The better part of every summer. Mom worked in the store when she and Dad were running things, so Gran kept an eye on us younger kids during the workday." She stopped to study several ears on a stalk. She gently peeled back a few of the yellow silks to study the kernels. "We always had so much fun we wound up staying overnight. There was always something to do. Trees to climb. Horses to ride. Adventures to go on."

"I can picture it." He held out the basket for her when she picked an ear. "That must have been an idyllic way to grow up."

"I think so."

He could see his future. As Rebecca picked corn ears, his heart dreamed of summers tending a garden of their own. Of horses in a field for their kids to ride. He saw a happy marriage and a good life to come with the woman who emerged from the cornstalks with the wind in her hair and similar dreams in her eyes.

Chapter Thirteen

Chad had the best evening with Rebecca. Gran, as he had been invited to call her, was a sweetheart of a lady who had kept them all laughing with one story after another of Rebecca as a little girl. She had even dug out the photo albums and he hadn't been surprised to see the little girl Rebecca had been with the pixie's face and brown ringlet curls. Lauren, who lived down the road, had come home around dessert time and had joined in.

Even the ride back to town was fun. He and Rebecca talked about everything and at the same time nothing at all. He had never laughed so much. His face hurt from smiling. With every passing minute he spent with her, he grew more in love with her.

"Oh, I've got a text message." She pulled

her phone out of her purse and studied it. "It's from Danielle. I'm babysitting, per usual, on Friday night, and she said you would be welcome to come, too. I can't imagine that would be your idea of a fun time, so I won't hold you to it."

"As a matter of fact I can't think of a better way to spend a Friday night." He slowed the truck and flicked on the turn signal. "I'd like to meet more of your family. Your niece and nephew sound great."

"I adore 'em." With her head bent and her hair falling softly to hide her face, she started typing a reply. "I'll let Danielle know it's a possibility."

There was a break in traffic and he turned into the complex. He had decided during supper tonight that he had to tell Rebecca the truth. He owed her that much. No, he owed her more than that. But how did he bring up such a painful subject?

Worse, how did he bring up something he knew might make her reject him? If she did that, then she would break more than his heart. He was all in; he had never felt tenderness so profound as the love he had for her.

"You do know what this means, don't you?" She looked up from her phone. "You and I have plans every night this week, including a family thing on Sunday."

"We're going to have to face what this is, you know." He risked a glance at her. "Apparently my no-dating policy and your friends-only policy did not stand up to the test."

"Are you kidding? They were worthless. Good ideas that didn't work for us."

"No, they didn't." He chuckled. How he had gotten lucky enough for God to bless him like this, he didn't know, but he never intended to take her for granted. "I hate to break this to you but it looks like we're dating."

"It doesn't just look that way. I think we are."

"Me, too." He pulled into his driveway and cut the engine. "Is that okay with you?"

"A tad. A smidgen. A pinch." She smiled, and without words he knew she meant it was more than okay.

He was attuned to her. He could feel the depth of her happiness. His answered prayer. "You're sending another text to your sister?"

"We're speculating why Ava was sick from work today," she told him as she went to open her door.

"Let me get that for you." He earned her smile as he circled around the truck, opened the door and took her hand.

This is what he wanted to spend the rest of his life doing. Holding her doors and making her life a little easier. Call him old-fashioned, but he felt that commitment down to his soul.

So, how did he tell her? Ephraim was home, so he couldn't ask her in. They would need some privacy to talk. Rebecca hopped lightly to the ground and he kept her hand as he closed the door.

How did he tell her? Did he start with the shocker: I spent eighteen months in juvie and a boot camp? Or did he start with a more subtle statement: after I got arrested for grand theft auto… It was hard to know. Either way, thinking of those days brought down a burden of shame—a shame he had to face. He had to risk losing her respect and her love. He had to believe her heart was big enough to understand.

"My grandmother is in love with you," Rebecca said as they crossed the road toward the mailboxes. "She gave me her approval."

"You know I sure liked her, too. I'm looking forward to meeting everyone in your family. I hope they have the same opinion about me because I care for you very much."

"I care for you, too." She blushed and looked down. She was shy.

"We are going to need a new policy."

"What kind of policy? After our failed attempts with the last ones, I'm a little leery of any others." Not that she wasn't happy with the outcome, but still.

"I understand, but hear me out. I would like us to be exclusive." He stuck by her side as they strolled up to the mailboxes. "Why don't we agree to a dating policy, just the two of us?"

"I'll agree with that." Bliss, that's what this joyful sunny feeling was. She was blissfully happy. What could be better than this man? He loved and respected her. He loved and respected her family. It had taken the right man to show her how wrong the wrong man had been for her.

"Good. Then it looks as if we have a deal, Rebecca." While his tone was light, his face was serious. "Would you mind if I came over? I have something I want to say to you alone."

"No one's around." She couldn't help joking a little. She tugged her mailbox open. "But come over. I was going to tackle some of my Bible study work tonight. Did you want to join me?"

"Absolutely."

She couldn't take her eyes off him. She

flipped through the envelopes. Credit card bill. Her cell phone bill. An unmarked envelope. She froze. What if it was from Chris? She checked the front and there was no stamp. There was no way to return it.

That's it. She tore open the flap, certain now. She had given Chris every opportunity to let go and move on, but she was done. She was going to give Caleb a call and find out about a restraining order.

There was one piece of paper inside. She unfolded it. It was a computer printout of a Web page. Of a Portland newspaper, she realized. There was a grainy black-and-white photograph of a much younger Chad standing in front of a courthouse with his lawyer and an older man, probably his grandfather. The bold letters above the picture and an article read, Plea Bargain Agreement Reached.

No, this couldn't be right. Her hands trembled. This had to be a mistake. A practical joke. Suddenly it came clear. This was Chris's idea of a cruel prank. Yes, that's what this was.

"You look upset, Rebecca. What's that you have there?"

She gazed up into his honest face. He looked like a man who could never do anything wrong. Her heart swelled two sizes with love for him. She went to fold up the paper, but her hands were shaking too hard.

"Let me see." His gentle baritone rumbled with reassurance, as if he could make anything right. He came up behind her and his hand steadied the top of the page.

"I can't believe he would make something up like this." The words felt torn from her throat. She had never felt so raw. Maybe because Chad wasn't saying anything. He wasn't denying it. He wasn't angry.

Sadness dug into his handsome face. "He didn't make this up, Rebecca."

"Wh-what?" Her ears had to be deceiving her.

"This is me. I did this. I stole a car and caused a wreck while I was joyriding."

Static buzzed in her head. His words sounded distant, as if he were on the other side of the complex instead of so close she could feel his cotton shirt against her elbow. No. This couldn't be true.

"I was lucky the folks I hit turned out to be all right." He took the paper and folded it back into thirds. "I, on the other hand, served an eighteen-month sentence and another year doing community service."

"Y-you were in jail?"

"Yes. I went through a boot camp program and juvie." He slipped the paper back inside the envelope she was still holding.

Chad was in jail. That thought rolled around inside her mind. Her blood went cold. She shivered in spite of the blazing sun harsh on her back. Chad had moved away and was watching her with sorrow on his face.

"This isn't how I wanted you to find out." His throat worked and he looked as if he were searching for words. "I was going to tell you."

"This was the complication you mentioned. The whopper of a mistake. This was what happened?" Why couldn't she still believe it? How foolish was she going to be? She could not deny this. She looked at Chad through new eyes. He was the seemingly perfect Prince Charming kind of guy, just like Chris. No, he was worse than Chris because Chris had never gone to jail.

To jail. Everything she knew about Chad fell like glass to the ground and shattered. The good and faithful man, the friend, the wholesome lifestyle and a forever kind of guy were gone. Tears burned behind her eyes. She took one long look at this stranger—at the man who had pretended to be something he wasn't. Her heart cracked and shattered, just like her illusions of him. She took a step away from him. It wasn't far enough.

"Rebecca, say something."

How could he stand there acting the same way? His eyes were dark with sorrow. His face beaming with sincerity. His shoulders were set straight and strong, as if he were stalwart enough to handle this, too.

"I don't know what to say." Her mind began to spin. Her throat stung. The pieces of her heart ached as if they were whole. "I thought— I don't know what I thought. Only that you were someone I could trust."

"I am that someone." He stepped toward her and held out his hand. He was reaching out for her.

"No." She shook her head. She crossed her arms over her heart. She backed away from him. It took all her courage to face him—to face the truth. "This was my mistake. I'm sorry, but we're done. Stay away from me, Chad."

"Rebecca, listen to me, please. I know we can work this out—"

She spun on her heel and fled. With every pound of her sneakers against the blacktop, she saw the last look on his face. He appeared as shattered as she felt.

The tears waited until she had closed and

locked her front door. Her knees gave out. She slid to the ground and buried her face in her hands. Nothing had ever hurt this much.

It's not because I love him, she argued with herself. It's because she trusted what he told her about his life. She had been duped. That was why she was in agony. Deception hurt.

Down deep, she knew it was more than that. She had loved him—honest and truly. She had thought he was someone else—someone who was a kindred spirit, a soul mate, her missing half.

What was wrong with her that she had fallen for another man capable of deceit? Why had she given her heart to another man with a reckless, self-destructive streak? And what was wrong with her that she was still in love with the person she'd wanted him to be?

Her phone chimed. It was a text message. Chad had sent just two words.

Forgive me.

If a little voice in her heart asked her to find forgiveness, she couldn't do it. She wouldn't. She wasn't going to repeat this unacceptable pattern in her life. She was not going to allow herself to be doomed to a series of bad relationships with men who were not what she deserved. She deserved honesty. She deserved respect. She deserved a man who loved her more than his own life.

Chad wasn't that man. That was her mistake, but it was one she wasn't going to make again. If the right man wasn't out there, then she was still going to be fine. She trusted where the Lord was leading her. She switched off her phone, swiped the damp from her eyes and bowed her head to pray.

"She's not answering me." This was killing him. Chad buried his face in his hands. He couldn't forget the sight of her running way from him—running, because walking away wouldn't be fast enough. She despised him. He had blown it big-time. She was never going to forgive him.

He wanted to blame her ex, who had probably looked up his name on Google and found the newspaper article. It was a simple thing to do. But the truth was, it was his own fault. He shouldn't have procrastinated. He should have told her sooner. Then maybe the outcome could have been different. But with the way she had found out, blunt like that and without a lick of explanation, she wasn't going to forgive him.

He didn't need an answer to his text

message to know that. He swiped his face, stood up and went to look out the sliding door. It wasn't the two plastic chairs and the plastic footstool he was seeing, but Rebecca's tiny and comfortable patio. How idyllic it had been sitting there barbecuing dinner and talking.

Looking back, he admitted the evening had been a dream because he had spent it with her.

No, he realized. It was something right out of his heart. It was a dream he hadn't even realized he wanted. It was as if God had looked into him, saw what he truly wanted and then set him on this path with Rebecca.

And I blew it. He leaned his forehead against the glass. He had lost her. Just like that. Everything had been going fine and then bam! It was all over.

"She needs time," Ephraim said from the couch where he was poking at the keyboard of his laptop computer. "She's a nice girl. You should have been the one to tell her. That's the real problem."

"That's part of it." But not all. His chest felt heavy, as if not a single molecule of air could fit in his lungs. He couldn't seem to breathe. He didn't want to. What he wanted was to go next door and talk until he made Rebecca understand.

"You've got to give her space, dude." Ephraim sounded extremely confident. "Trust me."

Trust the guy who had never been on a date? Chad shook his head. Ephraim might be inexperienced, but he did have three sisters. "You think she will forgive me?"

"I think you've got a shot at it. You see her tomorrow at work, right? Maybe that will be a good time to talk to her."

He nodded. He wasn't sure that Ephraim was right. He fisted his hands, frustrated. He wanted to do something to fix this. She was next door hurting. He had seen the pain in her eyes. She had lost more than her trust in him. She had lost her heart. He wanted to fix it for her. He wanted to make everything right. How could he leave things the way they were?

He couldn't, that's what. He grabbed his Bible and workbook from the edge of the counter and let himself out onto the patio. The late-evening air scorched him like a draft from an oven. He clutched his books and forced his feet to carry him through the grass and around the wooden partition that divided his yard from Rebecca's.

What was he going to tell her? He didn't have a clue. She was probably thinking the worst about him. She had probably come to some pretty harsh conclusions. Not that he blamed her a bit. He deserved it. He had done those things. Shame battered him as he wove around a few rosebushes and saw her through the glass door.

Sunlight streamed in the west windows, illuminating her as she knelt in prayer. She was deeper inside the house, with the front door at her back. From where he stood he had a perfect view of her. Her head was bent, her hands clasped, her soft face taut with emotion. She looked small and vulnerable. Everything within him wanted to comfort her. Every fiber of his being wanted to take away her pain.

If only she would give him that right. He waited, heart knocking and fear thick in his veins, as she finished praying. When she opened her eyes, her gaze went straight to him. There was no surprise on her lovely face. No flash of horror. It was as if she had known he was there all along.

He had to hold on to hope as she slowly climbed to her feet. He watched her self-control as she schooled her face, gathered a breath of air and paced through the living room. She removed the dowel and opened the door with controlled, tight movements. Her face was a mask of stoicism hiding every trace of pain.

He wasn't fooled. He could feel her agony as he could his own.

"I want to make this better," he told her. "I can explain."

"No." Her eyes winced, betraying her sadness and his fate. "It's too late, Chad."

"It can't be. I can fix this, Rebecca. I have to try." He set down the books on the table, determined to make her believe. He had to make her believe. "I'm in love with you. I know I should have told you sooner, but I'm still the same man. Everyone makes mistakes. That doesn't have to be who I am. I am someone different today. I need you to see that."

"How can I? All I see is that article. All I see is that you made me believe you were someone you're not." Her face crumpled into sheer heartbreak. "That's what Chris did. I don't want to be fooled like that again. I can't let myself."

"I understand that. You have every right to be unsure. You have every right to be upset and not want anything to do with me. But I'm asking you to please reconsider." His throat worked. He had run out of words, but not of heart. "Forgive me."

"How can I trust you?" Her knuckles turned white. "What will it be next? You have shown me the kind of man you are and I have to accept it. I'm not going to let this be a pattern in my life."

"Men who lie to you?"

"Men capable of causing harm." The color drained from her face. "I never told you about my real father. He was a violent man. He hurt my mother often."

Chad hung his head. It really was all over. He had never really had a chance with her. This had been wrong right from the start. There would be no future with her. No McKaslin family gatherings. No more bike rides. No vegetable gardens. No children with her smile.

He covered his eyes with his hand to hide the pain. Loss pounded through him like high tide cresting. He had been wrong to dream. "You think I'm like your father."

"I think trusting you again would be a mistake. I'm sorry, but I just can't look at you the same way."

He nodded. He couldn't blame her. A woman as nice and sweet as Rebecca wouldn't want a man with his past. He understood that. And now that he knew why, he could do the right thing—what he had to do.

He squared his shoulders and swept his books off the table. "Goodbye, Rebecca."

"Goodbye, Chad." She choked on a sob, but she held her chin high, firm in her decision.

"Tomorrow when I see you at work, I will be just another stranger." He wanted to reassure her that this would not be a repeat of her last relationship. He knew how to respect her wishes. What he didn't know how to do was to stop loving her.

"Thank you." She closed the door and replaced the dowel.

He couldn't remember how he got from her patio to his. He only knew the moment he had someplace private he bowed his head and let the loss hammer through him.

Chapter Fourteen

"Okay, Spence just left for an emergency church board meeting and the store is totally empty." Lauren popped around the end cap and dodged the book cart. "Why are you working on a weekday evening?"

Rebecca winced at Lauren's question. She looked up from the fiction shelves. "Spence called me in the middle of the day with a cry for help."

"That's not what I asked, and you know it." Lauren grabbed a book from the cart and glanced at the spine. She hunkered down to shelve the book. "You have been mysteriously hard to get a hold of ever since you called things off with Chad. You're not going tonight just to avoid him. I get it."

"It's still too fresh. Too painful." Rebecca

wished things had gone differently. She wished Chad was different. "The truth is I miss him. We had a lot of fun together."

"Oh, it was more than that." Lauren's kindness and caring made it hard to keep sensible.

Rebecca blinked hard, determined to keep her raw, broken feelings well hidden. "I'm pleading the fifth on that."

"You keep doing that, but one day you have to take the risk."

"What are you talking about?"

"I'm talking about really opening your heart and trusting in love."

"You sound like a greeting card commercial." Rebecca grabbed a book from the cart. "I did that. Twice."

"No, first you chose a guy who you could never be truly close to." Lauren slipped the book in place. "Then you fall for this great man. He's a real Mr. Dreamy. What do you do? When he gets too close and too real, you push him again."

"I had a good reason."

"I heard that reason. Danielle told me."

Footsteps padded on the other side of the aisle and Danielle rounded the corner. "Are you two over here talking without me?"

"Guilty." Rebecca gave up shelving entirely. "You two have been talking about me."

"Sure we have, because we love you." Danielle gave her a quick hug. "You still haven't forgiven Chad?"

"It isn't a matter of forgiveness." She looked at her sisters' faces, both lined with concern for her, and she faltered. How could she tell them what she felt? "You two have great guys. Dani, Jonas is about the most heroic man out there."

"He does have his moments," she agreed. "I am very blessed in my husband."

"And my Caleb is a two hundred on a scale of ten," Lauren chimed in. "But that doesn't mean I can't relate. I know something about being afraid to open your heart and honestly let someone in."

"Sure, I can't say that isn't a possibility." Rebecca knew her sisters had a point. "But Chad has made choices I can't accept. I can't see him the same anymore. He lied to me."

"He kept something painful hidden. Maybe because he's a bad person." Danielle sat down and stretched out on the carpet. "Or perhaps it was because it hurts to talk about it. I've been guilty of that kind of silence before."

"We all have," Lauren added.

Danielle kept going. "Sure, he made a mistake but you have to consider what he did afterward. That shows his character. Right?"

How did she explain to her wonderful sisters that it wasn't only Chad she no longer trusted, but herself? And maybe there was another reason, too. "So, how does a person who is afraid to let anyone too close fix that?"

"The way the rest of us do, sweetie." Danielle reached out and squeezed her hand. "You take a deep breath, lean on faith and go by heart. You try not to run away afraid and you remember that the chance to really love someone and be truly loved by them in return is a rare and precious gift. Don't let it pass you by because you're afraid of getting hurt. Life without love hurts so much more."

Rebecca hung her head, thinking that over. Okay, that was good advice. Today had been a hard day. She had pretended she didn't see Chad at morning worship. She had eaten alone on the garden bench. She had left work as soon as she possibly could so she wouldn't run the chance of seeing him in the parking lot.

"Do you know the worst of this?" she asked.

Both sisters shook their heads, no.

"I miss him. I feel as if I've lost a piece of

me somewhere and I'll never find it again. I'm afraid he's not the kind of man I can trust, I mean really trust, when push comes to shove. When times are tough. When I really need him to be there for me and do the right thing. And—"

"Did you hear what you just said?" Danielle interrupted gently. "You're afraid. You're the one."

"He's been in jail. Jail." Like her dad. Like Chris would be, if he had been caught. That scared her, whether she had a problem with trust or not.

"I think you should come with me." Lauren held out her hand. "Dani, is it okay if we use your computer?"

"You know it is." Danielle smiled as she rose to her feet. "That's enough of a break for me. I'll shelve these books for you."

"Aren't you supposed to be going home?" Rebecca stopped in her tracks.

"Yes, but my husband will understand. He knows something about how important true love is." Danielle waved her away. "Go on. Don't worry."

"We won't be long," Lauren promised, tugging Rebecca away. "You and I will do a little research. After all, if Chris can do it, so can we. Then you will know for sure if you can trust this man you love."

Chad hung up the phone. He'd had a rotten day, and it had just gotten worse. It had turned into a doom day. He stared at the fake wood grain of the kitchen table and gave thanks for shock. Because of it, right now he couldn't feel the hard blow of disappointment—although he would, in time, when the shock wore off.

"You don't look too happy," Ephraim commented from the counter where he was pouring two glasses of grape juice. "I take it whoever that was, it wasn't good news."

"No." To say the least. Chad rubbed the back of his neck. Tension was knotted up so tight, he could hardly move his head. "That was Pastor Marin. Someone e-mailed the newspaper article to half of the church members tonight."

"That's rough." Ephraim set down the juice bottle with a thunk. "Why would someone do that to you?"

"I have a few ideas." He wasn't the kind of man to accuse or lay blame, but he was pretty sure. "The board knows about my past, but because of this e-mailing now some of the parents of the day camp kids are alarmed. They don't want their children exposed to a man with a criminal record."

"That's harsh."

"I can't blame them." That was the thing. "This is where life gets tricky. That's in my past, but I'm afraid it's all that anyone is going to see about me. I can't go back and do over that bad decision. I would if I could."

"This is like a double whammy. First Rebecca, now this." Ephraim brought the glasses around the end of the counter and set them on the table. "I've known you since we were six. You've made one mistake in your life, and that's it. It shouldn't haunt you forever."

"Thanks, man." Ephraim's support meant a lot, but didn't change the truth that he would probably be asked to resign. This was a terrible blow, but losing Rebecca hurt more.

He took a sip of juice, but it was tasteless. His nerves were on high alert. Marin promised she would call as soon as the board meeting was over. He was man enough to take whatever outcome the board decided, but he sure loved working with the day camp program. He liked to think he was making a positive contribution.

"How did the day go with Rebecca?"

Chad shook his head. The last thing he wanted to do was to answer his buddy's question, but he knew Ephraim cared. He was a good friend. Chad ran his finger through the condensation beginning on the side of the glass. "She avoided me. When she couldn't avoid me, she ignored me."

"You and her were good together. I'm sorry."

"Me, too." He missed her. He missed hearing his phone chime and know there was a message waiting from her. He missed hearing that little trill of a laugh she had and the sound of her dulcet voice. And that was just the start. She had changed his life with her sweetness, and now he was never going to be the same without her.

And it was all his fault. He'd been a knucklehead. He should have made sure he had been the one to tell her. He could have eased her into the shock of it. He could have explained everything that happened afterward that had changed him from the reckless, rebellious teenager into the man he wanted to be one day. He had a long way to go, but he was determined to get there, God willing.

The doorbell rang. "It's probably for you, Ephraim. Maybe it's Elle next door."

"I doubt it. Have you noticed I've ditched the pocket protector—"

"Hey, you did."

"For all the good it's done. I have an ink stain on two of my shirts. No idea how to get it out." He stood, shaking his head. "I thought it might get me noticed, but no. That's probably someone selling lightbulbs or handing out pizza coupons."

"We could use pizza coupons," Chad pointed out, trying to lighten things a little.

Ephraim shot him a grin as he headed for the front door.

How had things gone from so great to so bad so fast? He rubbed a hand over his forehead. He was starting to get a tension headache. There had to be a reason for this, he figured. He wasn't going to get any more upset than he already was. He was going to trust that this was in God's hands, too, and it would all work out for the best.

Now, if he could get his nervous stomach and his broken heart to believe that, he would be in better shape. He took another swig of juice and tried not to think about the meeting or Rebecca.

Rebecca. He set the glass down. He felt so empty inside. He wondered what she was doing right now. Talking on the phone with one of her sisters? Stopping by the bookstore to pick up another book? Studying her Bible out on her back patio?

He missed her so much it hurt. Unable to stand it anymore, he pushed away from the table. Maybe he ought to finish his daily study, too. Do something constructive, at least. Maybe that would keep his mind off what he had already lost.

"Hey, Chad." Ephraim called from the foyer. "It's someone for you."

"For me?" He couldn't imagine who. He changed directions in midstride and paced down the hall. He followed the sound of Ephraim's voice as he spoke with whoever was outside.

A woman's voice answered him, gentle and dulcet and familiar.

Rebecca. Surprise jolted through him. He put speed into his walk, even as doubt crept in. It couldn't be her. Maybe it was someone who sounded similar to her. There was no way she was going to forgive him. He knew that.

"Hi, Chad." She stood on the other side of the door, looking amazing in jeans and a summery blue top. Her hair was down, and she seemed at peace.

His heart gave a little kick of hope. Hold on, he couldn't go leaping to assumptions. She could be here for a dozen reasons and every one of them had nothing to do with giving him a second chance.

"I heard about the e-mailing. Lauren got one of the e-mails." She was holding a paper bag by the paper handles. Her tone was almost apologetic and neutral.

The little hope he had fizzled. This was just like at work today. She was being polite, that was all. Crushed, he gathered his courage and held back his disappointment. There would be time to feel that later, when she wasn't around. He didn't want her to know that he was still foolishly hoping.

"I'm sorry." Her sincerity was unmistakable. "I know how much this volunteer work means to you."

He nodded, not really wanting to talk about it. He had taken just about his quota of pain for the day. But then it hit him what she had said. Surely he hadn't misunderstood. "Y-you do know?"

"That article about your plea bargain wasn't the only article about you in the Portland paper." There was no hint on her pretty face.

He didn't know what she was trying to tell him. Was she talking about the arrest? The reports on his hospitalization? On minor injuries of the people hurt in the other car? Adrenaline jolted through him. How could this get even worse? And why did it have to be right now, when he was down, that she'd come to bring up more of those painful pieces of his past?

"I can't do this, Rebecca." It was like a bullet to the chest. He grasped the door frame to hold himself steady. "I don't want to rehash the past. It tortures me. I thank God every day that I was the one seriously hurt in that accident and not the people I slammed into. I can't do enough to make up for that. I have to leave it in the past. It hurts too much."

She stared at him with her wide, luminous eyes. It was impossible to read the wince of emotion on her beloved face. It was impossible because he loved her still. Even knowing he could never have the right to call her his, the love in his heart stubbornly lived.

"I didn't come here to cause you more hurt," she said in her quiet, gentle way. "Did you get my text message?"

"What message?" He'd checked his cell phone about an hour ago, around the time he'd found out about the mass e-mailing. There hadn't been a message then, and he'd muted it. He was already pulling his cell out of his jeans pocket and checked the screen.

Sure enough there was a message. His hands trembled as he hit the read button.

Yes, she'd written.

Chapter Fifteen

"You forgive me?"

Rebecca studied the man standing in front of her. His eyes were shadowed and tension had cut creases into his handsome face. She longed to reach out and comfort him. She wished she knew how to make everything all right for him.

"I understand why you didn't tell me first off." A tiny curl of panic fluttered within her but she didn't buckle. She had come here with her heart wide-open. Sure it was scary, but so was the thought of living her life without this man. She gathered her courage and took the risk. "I understand why you wanted to wait to tell me until I knew you better."

He nodded and pocketed his phone. His eyes saddened, taking her hopes with him.

Had her forgiveness come too late? She desperately hoped not. She clutched the bag until her knuckles were white. This wasn't easy. She cleared her throat and finished what she'd come to say. "I understand that you are more today than the boy who made those poor decisions."

He hung his head. "I don't understand. You said you can't see me the same way anymore."

"I read all the articles, Chad. Every last one." She thought she felt hope rise up, but she couldn't be sure. "You were in intensive care for three weeks. You made full restitution to the family and to the man whose car you stole. You voluntarily turned yourself in. You chose a plea bargain when your family could have afforded the best in defense attorneys. You chose to face the consequences of your actions instead of trying to get out of them."

"That's true." He met her gaze. "You have to know that I've changed because of that. In a way, I thank God for it because it saved me. My bad decision put me on this path. I will never forget it. I will never repeat those patterns in my life because it's my choice."

"I read that in your article, the one that was published in a Christian teen magazine."

"Oh, you found that, too?"

Anyone could see his modesty and the way

he faintly blushed. But she knew him well enough to read the shame there, too. He had made good of his life in spite of where he had been heading. Danielle was right. His actions did show his character.

"Lauren is a whiz with the computer," she explained. "It takes a real man to admit his mistakes, to make amends and accept the consequences and to build his life anew."

"You make me sound noble, and that's not true, Rebecca. I try to do the right thing. That's all. That's who I am now and who I will always be." He came closer, into the brush of sunlight. "I promise I will always do my best to do what's right. I hope you can believe that."

"I do." The backs of her eyes began to burn. "I know that about you now."

"You do." He closed his eyes for a brief moment. "That's a relief."

They smiled together and there it was, that click of emotional connection. It was like an anchor securing her heart with his. It was like a nod from heaven saying, here's the one. She felt alive with hope and thankfulness.

This wasn't a man who made a habit of secrets and bad choices. No, Chad was the kind of man she could trust with her heart for now. And for always.

"I'm sorry for how I reacted." She steeled her spine. "I shouldn't have pushed you away until I had all of the story. That was my fault, all mine."

"Did you push me away?" He reached out and brushed a satin lock of hair from her eyes. "I didn't notice. I was so busy worrying about how I hurt you and blew my chance with you."

"I pushed you away." This she knew for certain. Even now a part of her wanted to take a step away from him, to keep a safe distance between them. It was how she had always been. She always kept everyone at a safe distance. She rarely opened up in a truly deep and personal way, even to her sisters. She had a lot of acquaintances, but not a lot of close friends. Chad had gotten closer to her than anybody had.

It scared her. Letting him close meant having to trust him with her heart and with all the fragile pieces of her spirit.

"How do I know you aren't going to do that again?" he asked.

She rolled her eyes. "I deserve that. You can't know how hard this is for me."

"Sure I can. For true love to work, both people have to take down their shields and set aside their defenses and trust that the other person will handle them with care. You've had men in your life who did not do that."

"That's true." She reached out with one hand to take his. She twined their fingers together. Her soul sighed. Her spirit felt complete. The broken shards of her heart became whole. "Danielle told me that the chance to really love someone and be truly loved by them in return is a rare and precious gift. You're worth the risk, Chad."

"I'm so very glad you think so." The sadness faded from his eyes and the worry from his face. "You are worth the risk, too."

"Then I guess this means our dating-only-each-other policy is back in effect?"

"That would be my greatest wish." He kissed her hand like a prince in a fairy tale. The sunlight chose that moment to deepen into a gentle rose-colored glow.

It was as if the world had changed. As if it would always be beautiful because of the love they shared. She did love this man, more than was sensible and more than was wise. Her soul sighed at his nearness. She was no longer afraid.

"Guess what's in the bag," she invited him. "It's something I know you will like."

"I'm afraid to guess." There were his

dimples, digging deep. His smile was her favorite sight.

She opened the bag and pulled out the box. "Popsicles. If you'll notice they are—"

"Grape," he finished. "My favorite kind."

"Mine, too," she added. "Someone once told me a grape Popsicle has very special properties—"

"They tend to cement important relationships." He completed her sentence again.

"I suppose this means we're back to being friends?"

"No." He leaned forward to press a sweet kiss to her forehead. "We're more than friends. We're best friends. I've heard that true love starts with a fantastic friendship."

"Where have you heard that?" She laughed as he dropped a tender kiss on the tip of her nose. Very sweet. "This friendship thing is all I've heard from my mom, my sisters and even my pastor."

"I heard it from my grandfather. He had the best sense of humor. He and my grandmother were always laughing. I always wanted a relationship like that, one that was a joy and a blessing."

"Me, too." Maybe there was more to this friendship thing than she had first thought.

She was grateful to God for leading her to Chad. Very grateful.

She went up on tiptoe for their first kiss. It was chaste and tender and sweet, just as true love should be.

Epilogue

It was a frosty November day and snow was falling. Rebecca stomped her feet to get the blood flowing. She was dressed for the cold, but after spending all day on the ski slopes even her bone marrow was cold.

"Let's go in for a steaming hot cup of cocoa," Chad suggested as he stowed their skis outside the mountain lodge. "I'm in the mood to celebrate."

"You mean celebrate our first time skiing together?"

"No, while that's been great, I've got something else to celebrate." He straightened and took her gloved hand. It felt wonderful and natural to be at his side and crunching through the deep snowpack with him.

"Oh, you have some news you haven't

shared with me." She let him lead her toward a private spot near a grove of evergreens. "You received the best score on your term paper, right? Or did you get another article published?"

"Neither. No, what I have to celebrate is something that means much more to me than that." He had a mysterious smile on his handsome face. "In fact, nothing on this earth could mean more."

"I'm clueless." She could read the excitement in his eyes and the joy on his face. "Whatever this is, it's really good news, isn't it?"

"I'm sure hoping it will be. I don't know for sure yet."

She frowned. He wasn't making sense. "What are you talking about? Chad, what's going on?"

"You can't guess?" He took her left hand and knelt at her feet.

"Y-you're proposing?"

"Of course we can only celebrate if you say yes." He gave her his charming, full-wattage smile, the one that showed his dimples. He pulled a small black box from his parka pocket. "So, will you, Rebecca? Will you marry me? Will you do me the great honor of becoming my wife?"

Tears stung her eyes, blurring his beloved face and the beautiful majesty of the high mountains. "If I marry you, then that means you and I will spend the rest of our lives together."

"Yes, I understand that's the way it works. Through sickness and health. Through good times and hard times." His grin faded, and he was rock-solid sincerity. "I vow to always love you and treat you well, Rebecca. You are my heart."

"You are mine." Her throat was burning. Her mind was spinning. "I didn't expect this. You're not out of school yet."

"I don't want to wait. I'm sure. I will love you forever. Say yes and let me prove it to you."

"Yes." She blinked hard, trying to bring him into focus. "I love you, Chad, forever and ever. I can't wait to marry you."

Her hand was shaking as he took the ring from the box. This was it, the moment she hadn't let herself dream of. The last few months had been blissful. They had spent every day together and she had never been so happy.

Nor, she knew, had he. He was still volunteering for the church and had developed a much-respected reputation there. He was enjoying school. And the time they spent together, whether it was watching an old movie on the couch or outdoors on a day like this, felt like paradise.

What everyone said was true. The best kind of romantic love was built on the foundation of friendship.

"We're officially engaged." He slipped the ring on her fourth finger. "Is that your cell phone ringing?"

"It's probably one of my sisters. I'm going to let it go to voice mail. I want to keep you all to myself for a little while. You promised me hot chocolate, buddy."

"I'm a man who keeps his promises." He rose and gathered her in his strong arms. "I promise to make you happy, Rebecca."

"I know you will, because I already am." She laid her cheek against his chest. She felt safe and secure and loved. She could see her dreams coming true. A happy marriage. Children one day. A good life spent with him, her best friend, laughing all the way.

She took a moment to give thanks that God had led her to Chad—her perfect man.

* * * * *

*Don't miss Jillian Hart's
next Inspirational romance,
HIS HOLIDAY HEART,
available from Love Inspired
November 2008.*

Dear Reader,

Thank you so much for choosing *Her Perfect Man*. I hope you enjoyed reading Rebecca's and Chad's story as much as I did writing it. Throughout the third McKaslin story, Rebecca had been in love with Chris, until things between them went terribly wrong. Now in her story, she is picking up the pieces, trying to figure out where the Lord is leading her, and determined to stay away from romance again. Love hurts too much, she believes. Until Chad walks into her life with his Prince Charming ways and offers a friendship she cannot say no to. I hope Rebecca and Chad's faithful journey from friendship to love touches your heart.

Wishing you the best of blessings,

Jillian Hart

QUESTIONS FOR DISCUSSION

1. At the beginning of the story, how would you describe Rebecca's character? What are her weaknesses and her strengths? How has her past influenced who she is?

2. When Rebecca meets Chad, what is her first impression of him? What character traits does Chad reveal?

3. How does Rebecca's "no date" policy change throughout the story? Why does it change?

4. Rebecca is struggling with setting aside her tendency to worry and give her problems up to prayer. How is this evident? Have you ever struggled with this?

5. Chad is struggling with a mistake he made in his youth, one he regrets. How do you know that his regret is sincere?

6. How is God's leading evident in the story?

7. How does Rebecca resolve her worries over her past and repeating past patterns in her life?

8. Chad has worked hard to rebuild himself and his life anew. What does this say about his character? How do you know this will be a lasting change?

9. By the end of the story, how has Rebecca's character changed, and why?

10. How important are the themes of forgiveness and second chances? What are your experiences with forgiveness and second chances?

11. How does Rebecca's family strengthen and support her?

12. How would you describe Rebecca's faith? Chad's faith? How are each strengthened through the story?

Love Inspired® SUSPENSE

RIVETING INSPIRATIONAL ROMANCE

Watch for our new series of
edge-of-your-seat suspense novels.
These contemporary tales
of intrigue and romance
feature Christian characters
facing challenges to their faith...
and their lives!

Steeple
Hill®

Visit:
www.SteepleHill.com

Love Inspired.
HISTORICAL

INSPIRATIONAL HISTORICAL ROMANCE

Engaging stories of romance,
adventure and faith,
these novels are set in
various historical periods
from biblical times
to World War II.

NOW AVAILABLE!

**Steeple
Hill**®

For exciting stories that reflect traditional values,
visit:
www.SteepleHill.com